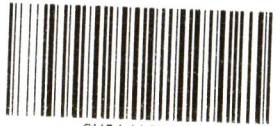

BROGAN
TAKES TOLL

L.D. TETLOW

A Black Horse Western

ROBERT HALE · LONDON

ISBN 0 7090 4835 1

Robert Hale Limited
Clerkenwell House
Clerkenwell Green
London EC1R 0HT

Photoset in North Wales by
Derek Doyle & Associates, Mold, Clwyd.
Printed in Great Britain by
St Edmundsbury Press Ltd, Bury St Edmunds, Suffolk.
Bound by WBC Bookbinders Ltd, Bridgend, Glamorgan.

ONE

Brogan heard the crack of the rifle shot a split second before he felt the bullet singe his left ear; instinctively he fell off his horse, making sure he landed behind a large rock and lay still, feigning death.

He was aware of a trickle of blood beginning to ooze down his cheek, but he made no attempt to wipe it off, even when the inevitable flies began to cluster on the spot. There had not been a fly to be seen up until then but fresh blood soon brought them zooming in. He had not tried to hide himself completely either, he knew that his legs could still be seen by his assailant, whoever it was, but the more vulnerable parts of him were protected by the rock. As he had fallen, he had drawn his Colt which he now grasped in his hand under his body.

'I reckon I musta killed 'im!' a man's voice shouted.

'Sure looks like it,' agreed another voice. Still Brogan made no attempt to move. 'Looks like he was alone,' continued the second voice. 'Let's take a look.'

Brogan waited, listening to the shuffle of horses' hoofs along the dry, dusty trail and finally deciding that there were only two of them. Being shot at was nothing new to Brogan McNally, saddletramp, but there was usually a reason for it, but this time he had been taken completely by surprise; there was no reason at all as far as he knew, but obviously the two men approaching him did have their reason. The horses stopped a few yards away and he heard the men dismount, but he still feigned death. The scrape of leather on the dry earth and stones became louder, eventually stopping alongside him.

Through slitted eyelids, he made out two men, neither particularly young and who did not give the impression of being outlaws or even drifters like himself. The sight of the blood on Brogan's ear and cheek seemed to convince the men that he was dead and they returned their guns to their holsters.

'Sure don't recognize 'im,' said the shorter of the two, who also appeared to be the elder. 'But that don't mean nothin'.'

'See if'n he's got any identification,' said the other man, who despite his apparent age, looked a powerful man. The first man bent down and turned Brogan over.

'The name's McNally!' Brogan hissed as the man started backwards, staring into the barrel of Brogan's Colt. The second man made a movement towards his holster and cried out in agony as a shot shattered the bones of his hand. 'That was kinda foolish!' grinned Brogan, sitting up. 'I could just as easy've killed you!' The two men stared in helpless terror. 'Only reason I didn't,' continued Brogan, 'was 'cos I'd kinda like to know why you tried to kill me. I'm sorta funny 'bout things like that, I like to know if you got a grudge against me or I done somethin' wrong.'

'You oughta know why!' grunted the older looking man.

'Mister!' Brogan sighed, 'if I knew, I wouldn't be askin', would I? Now, let's hear some straight talkin' before I do decide to blow away your brains, if you got any that is.' The two men looked at each other, obviously puzzled.

'Cartwright!' muttered the injured man, attempting to wrap a handkerchief around his injured hand. 'Clem Cartwright.'

'Clem Cartwright!' said Brogan. 'An' just who might this Clem Cartwright be?'

'You don't know?' asked the injured man, not having much success with the handkerchief.

Brogan sighed and shook his head. 'Like I already said, I wouldn't be askin' if'n I knew, would I?'

'You gotta know!' insisted the first man. 'Where you been livin' lately? You just rode outta the pass, nobody goes in or out of Apache River Pass without Cartwright's say-so.'

'Mister!' Brogan hissed. 'I'm gettin' kinda fed up with all this. I'll tell you just one more time, I ain't never heard of no Clem Cartwright an' I ain't ever heard of this Apache River Pass until now. Sure, I came through some pass or other, but I didn't see nobody, I didn't hear nobody an' I didn't smell nobody!' The two men looked hard at each other, very puzzled. 'So I say again, what gives with you tryin' to kill me?'

'Y'know,' said the first man, 'I kinda believe you.

I don't reckon you is with Cartwright.'

'Now we're beginnin' to make some sorta progress!' said Brogan.

'How the hell did you manage to get through without him seein' you then?' demanded the injured man, suspiciously.

'Easy,' laughed Brogan, 'my old horse just kept on puttin' one foot in front of the other.'

'It don't make sense!' the man muttered.

'Nothin' don't make no sense!' agreed Brogan. 'Not that I'm that bothered, it ain't my problem, but what the hell is all this about?'

The first man took the handkerchief off his companion and began to tie it round the injured hand. 'Clem Cartwright is an outlaw,' he explained, ''bout as bad as they come I reckon. Him an' his men is holdin' the town to ransom …'

'Town! What town?' Brogan interrupted.

'Apache Falls, 'bout four or five miles further on.'

'Good,' said Brogan. 'I was beginnin' to wonder if I'd find a town or a tradin' post, I need me some fresh supplies. You say this Cartwright is holdin' the town to ransom, just how the hell can he do that?'

The injured man scowled at Brogan. 'I ain't sure if'n I believe you or not …'

'Mister!' snapped Brogan. 'I don't give a damn what you believe. It sure as hell don't matter none to me if this Cartwright is holdin' the town to ransom or not. I reckon I got far better things to do than stand here jawin' to two old men what don't seem to know what's what.' He strode over to his horse, taking care to keep his Colt in his hand

and in the view of the men, mounted and rode off before either of them could say anything else.

As he rode, he thought back to his journey through the pass. He had told the truth when he had said that he had not seen or heard anyone, but he had had the distinct feeling of being watched. He had tried to place his watcher but had been unable to narrow it down beyond three possible spots. But, they had left him alone and he had not given it much further thought.

The town of Apache Falls loomed ahead of him and he could see how it got the 'Falls' part of its name. About three or four hundred yards from the town, the nearby river – he guessed it was the same one which flowed through the pass, although he had not followed it, taking the shorter route across country – cascaded in a series of waterfalls.

It was a town like many others, possibly a little larger than some and from the number of cows around, seemed to be a cattle town. Curious eyes followed his progress along the wide main street – another indication that it was a cattle town – and he knew that he was being watched by the sheriff, the flash of the metal star in the sunlight on the chest of a tall, muscular man had told him that much from over a hundred yards away.

Brogan's immediate need was for flour and salt, although he would take the opportunity to stock up on his other needs and he pulled up outside a general store, about forty yards short of the sheriff's office. He ignored the sheriff's steady gaze, but he had already formed an opinion of the man. This sheriff had an air of authority and self assurance about him which a great many others did not and, from the way he wore his gun, Brogan also knew that he could use it. The sheriff of Apache Falls did not look like a man to be trifled or even argued with.

As he had ridden in, he had also been aware of the two men he had met following him and as he entered the store, he saw them on the edge of town and knew that they would be reporting to the sheriff. Generally speaking, Brogan and sheriffs did not mix very well and he felt no desire at all to test himself against this particular one, so, he would buy his supplies and get the hell out of it.

The storekeeper looked a little surprised to see Brogan. 'You musta come through Apache River Pass ...'

'So I been told,' Brogan interrupted. 'I need some flour an' salt, a small bag of each an' I guess I might as well stock up on beans an' salt beef ...'

'Ain't got no salt beef,' said the storekeeper, deciding not to press or question the stranger.

'No salt beef!' exclaimed Brogan. 'There's hundreds of cows out there an' you say you got no salt beef!'

'Nope,' said the storekeeper, blandly. 'No salt beef. I got some bacon, that's all.'

Brogan examined some small sides of smoked bacon. 'I'll take this.' He indicated one. 'Prefer salt beef though.'

'If you really want salt beef, I got some,' said the storekeeper, 'but it ain't cured proper yet.'

'It ain't no use if it ain't cured proper,' said Brogan, taking a box of cartridges off a shelf. 'An' these!' He leant on the counter and stared at the storekeeper, who flinched under his gaze. 'So, I come through this pass. The other two I met seemed surprised as well – what gives?'

'Nobody goes through Apache River Pass unless Cartwright lets 'em,' replied the storekeeper.

'I just did,' said Brogan. The door opened and the sheriff walked in.

'You did what?' came the demand.

'Rode through this pass what everybody says I shouldn't've been able to,' said Brogan.

'So I hear,' said the sheriff. 'Old Aaron's nursin' a mighty sore hand on account of you.'

'Old Aaron should think himself lucky he can still nurse his hand,' said Brogan, with a wry smile. 'He could just as easy've been dead.'

'Yeh,' the sheriff sighed. 'I heard him an' Jake tried to kill you. How come you didn't kill 'em, seems you had cause enough?'

'What the hell I wanna kill old men for?' asked Brogan. 'Mind you an inch closer an' I'd be buzzard meat now.' He indicated his ear, the blood now clotted over the small wound. ''Sides, who would've believed me?'

'I reckon I would've.' The sheriff smiled. 'They is a stupid pair of critters. Just 'cos they was in the cavalry they reckon they know how to fight anythin' and everyone. They took it on themselves to act as guards over the town. I tried to talk 'em out of it but they wouldn't listen to sense.'

'Better tell 'em any strangers that come through ain't necessarily outlaws,' said Brogan. 'Maybe next time, if there is a next time, they won't meet someone who is so kindly disposed as I am. Most'd just shoot 'em an' think nothin' of it.'

'I already told 'em,' smiled the sheriff. 'Mind you, they got a point, just how in the hell did you get through?'

'I'll tell you the same as I told them,' replied Brogan. 'It was easy. My old horse just put one foot in front of another.'

'Didn't nobody try an' shop you?'

'Nope, didn't see nobody, but I did have this feelin' I was bein' watched, an' my feelin's ain't never wrong.'

The sheriff grinned. 'Then I can only guess they realized you was only a drifter an' decided you wasn't worth the bother.' He sniffed the air. 'Yeh, saddletramp, they had no need to bother.'

'Then I reckon that was about the only time bein' a saddletramp has worked in my favour!' laughed Brogan.

'Plannin' on stayin' long?' asked the sheriff.

Brogan laughed again. 'From the way you said that, I guess I ain't. No, I'll pick me up these supplies an' be on my way. It's OK, Sheriff, your town won't have to put up with my smell for too long.'

The sheriff smiled wryly. 'From the way old Aaron tells it, you ain't no mean gun; he swears you knew exactly what you was doin'.'

'Oh, I did,' said Brogan, a little boastfully. 'I always know.'

'Yeh, I reckon you do at that,' said the sheriff. 'Rare combination that, a saddletramp what can handle a gun. I got me this feelin' that makes you a dangerous man.'

'I'm only dangerous to them what asks for it,'

said Brogan.

'Which makes you doubly dangerous,' observed the sheriff. 'So where you headed? Since you come in from the south I'd say you was headed north.'

Brogan shrugged. 'North, south, east or west, it don't make no difference to me. I ain't goin' nowhere's in particular.'

'Then it don't matter to you if you heads back south again?'

Again Brogan shrugged. 'I guess not, but I already seen what's that way. Why'd you say that?'

''Cos south is the only way outta here,' said the sheriff. 'West an' north there's Apache Canyon, three or four hundred feet sheer. East is more'n two hundred miles of desert with no water, no nothin', just rock an' sand.'

'There's gotta be a way either across or round the canyon,' said Brogan.

'Oh sure,' smiled the sheriff. 'There's two ways. North, the canyon ends in the desert an' from there you get desert in all directions for a couple of hundred miles, an' don't count on followin' the river, it just kinda fades out. West, the canyon ends up in the hills not far from the pass; an' the hills an' the pass is Cartwright territory.'

'So's south from what I hear,' said Brogan.

'Oh yeh, that's true,' said the sheriff.

'I see now how this Cartwright is holdin' the town to ransom. He controls the only way in an' out. How do supplies get through?'

The sheriff laughed. 'He charges a toll. It seems to suit him; easy money. He charges a hundred dollars for each supply wagon an' any of the goods he fancies, ten dollars for each horse an' rider an' five dollars a head for cattle.'

'An' you pay?' exclaimed Brogan.

'If folk wanna live they ain't got much choice,' said the sheriff.

Brogan stared at the sheriff in amazement. 'So why not just wire for a US marshal or even the cavalry?'

'Because we ain't got no telegraph no more, wire must've been cut down in the pass. 'Sides, the marshal is over a hundred miles west an' the nearest army post is fifty miles beyond that.'

Brogan shook his head. 'I seen lotsa sheriffs in my time, all shapes an' sizes; some good men, a lot of 'em bad. I been hounded outa more towns than I can count on account of what I am. But you look like a man what knows how to handle himself. I don't reckon you is scared of a few outlaws. Couldn't you do somethin'?'

The sheriff smiled. 'I ain't scared an' I could handle it, but not on my own. We did try but you musta seen the pass, a handful of men could hold up a whole army an', as far as I know, Cartwright's got about twenty-four men. After we tried to flush 'em out, he burned down two homesteads an' threatened to burn down the whole town. Folks kinda backed off after that, 'ceptin' old Aaron an' Jake, but even the three of us couldn't hope to handle 'em.'

'Surely somebody's heard about all this, 'specially if folk can get through the pass by payin' a toll.'

'If they have, they sure ain't bothered to do nothin',' said the sheriff. 'I guess they think they got enough of their own problems. This is only some hick town they ain't never heard of, so why should they bother? 'Sides, it's only been goin' on for two months.'

'Can't go on for ever,' said Brogan.

'No, guess not,' agreed the sheriff. 'But it's already caused a cash shortage an' folk can't afford to ship livestock or goods in or out for much longer.'

'An' when they can't pay, Cartwright'll move on,' said Brogan.

'Maybe,' smiled the sheriff. 'But he's a wanted man, as are most, if not all his cronies. They is safe enough up there for quite a long time.'

'So why don't you or someone ride out, pay your toll, go to the marshal an' tell him?'

'Oh sure,' smiled the sheriff. 'I reckon someone could do just that, but not me; Cartwright's already made it plain I ain't allowed to leave. Even if we did get a message through to the marshal an' he did come with a posse, he wouldn't stand no chance of flushin' Cartwright outa the hills or the pass. He's already said he'll burn out every wagon that tries to get through an' kill everybody what comes an' goes through the pass if the marshal arrives, an' believe me, he could too. So, folks ain't prepared to take the chance, not yet anyhow.'

'Then it seems you got you a problem.' Brogan shrugged. 'Me, I got me a problem too. Seems north an' west is out, so I got me a choice of crossin' the desert or goin' back south.'

'There's more'n two hundred miles of desert,' reminded the sheriff, 'an' not a single drop of water anywheres.'

'I reckon I could survive that,' said Brogan.

'There's always cactus an' lizards, but I don't reckon my old horse would stand it.'

'That's for sure,' agreed the sheriff. 'Well, I got work needs doin', just thought I'd let you know what you is up against.'

'Thanks!' grinned Brogan. 'Just the kinda news I wanted.' The sheriff nodded and left the store. 'How much I owe you?' he asked the storekeeper.

'Seven dollars!' came the reply.

'Seven dollars!' exclaimed Brogan.

'Yeh, seven dollars,' said the storekeeper. 'I got me a lot of overheads to cover.'

Brogan laughed. 'I guess you have at that, but seven dollars!'

'Take it or leave it,' rasped the storekeeper.

Brogan pulled a crumpled ten-dollar note from his pocket. 'I guess I got no choice. Is there anywhere my horse can get a feed?'

'There's a livery stable top end of town.'

'An I guess the livery stable's got a lotta overheads too.'

'We all got big overheads,' the storekeeper grumbled. Brogan laughed dryly and picked up his three dollars change and took his supplies outside and put them in his saddle-bags.

He soon found the livery stable and, as he had expected, the blacksmith too had 'Lotsa overheads,' but Brogan felt that his horse deserved a good feed she had only eaten rough grass for over a week. He left her in a stall, munching happily on her feed and went to the saloon.

'Beer!' he called to the bartender.

'One dollar!' replied the bartender, solemnly, waiting to see if Brogan still wanted the drink.

'Dollar!' sighed Brogan. 'I know, don't tell me, you got a lot of overheads too.' The bartender nodded. 'OK, one dollar, I reckon I can just about afford that.'

'Then you is one of the lucky ones,' muttered the bartender. 'Drinkin' is the one thing most folk've given up round here.'

'At a dollar for a beer, I ain't surprised,' retorted Brogan. 'Anyhow, it should save the sheriff a bit of work, ain't nobody can afford to get drunk. You lived here long?'

'Since I was a boy,' came the grunted reply. 'Always been a good town, but I'm beginnin' to have second thoughts right now. Only trouble is we got all our money tied up in the property an' I don't reckon we is gonna find too many buyers right now. I guess I'm better off than most, I ain't got no mortgage to repay; most the others, the farmers an' ranchers have, an' they're beginnin' to worry about bein' repossessed.'

'I don't reckon anybody got that much need to worry; it can't go on for ever,' said Brogan, casually. 'This Cartwright is gonna move on when he's got all he can outa this town.'

'Maybe!' grunted the bartender. 'Maybe not. Even if he does, it's a case of when an' I don't reckon the banks is gonna be too sympathetic: they never have been yet; they ain't exactly renowned for waitin' for their money.'

'Then it looks like you all got problems,' said Brogan, taking a sip of his expensive beer. 'Me, I'm headin' outa here.'

'I hear tell you came in through the pass,' said the bartender. 'Only way you is gonna leave is back through it.'

'So I heard,' said Brogan. 'Seems a crazy place to build a town if you ask me. Where'd this river just outside town end up?'

'Starts in the pass an' ends in the canyon.'

'No way down?' asked Brogan.

'Sure, just step off the edge,' smiled the bartender. 'Maybe you'd make it on your own, but there's no way you can get your horse across.'

'You reckon you've lived here all your life, so you must know the territory better'n anyone. If you was anythin' like I was as a kid, you musta done some explorin'. Surely there's another way out.'

'Nothin' to stop you tryin' to cross the desert,' replied the bartender, 'but unless you got the means of carryin' plenty of water, that's out. A couple of families have gone that way an' as far as I know they made it, but they had wagons an' barrels of water for their horses. It ain't just the lack of water out there; in the day I don't reckon there's a place on earth that's hotter, an' at night it freezes your balls off. If you was ridin' a mountain goat you'd probably make it across the canyon, but you ain't.'

'Then it looks like I gotta go back through the pass,' said Brogan. 'I didn't have no trouble comin' in, maybe I won't have no trouble gettin' out.'

'I wouldn't count on it,' smiled the bartender. 'I don't know why you wasn't stopped on the way through before, but I can't see you not bein' stopped on the way back. It'll cost you ten dollars.'

'An' what happens if I ain't got the ten dollars?'

'Then they take whatever they fancy. Maybe

they'll take your ten dollars an' let you through, maybe they'll want more.'

'I reckon I can afford the ten dollars,' said Brogan, finishing his beer and leaving the saloon. Outside he met the sheriff.

'You on your way?' asked the sheriff.

'Just leavin',' nodded Brogan. 'P'raps as well, I couldn't afford the prices in this town much longer.'

'Best of luck!' said the sheriff, genuinely.

'That's gotta go down as another first!' grinned Brogan. 'A sheriff wishin' me the best of luck.'

'We ain't all bad,' smiled the sheriff.

'Want me to get a message to anyone, such as the marshal?'

'You can if you want,' agreed the sheriff, 'but I don't reckon he'll take that much notice. Other folk have told him, or at least they promised to, but nothin's happened yet.'

'I ain't makin' no promises,' said Brogan, 'but if I run into anyone, I'll tell 'em.'

'I'll believe it if it happens,' the sheriff smiled.

Brogan returned to the livery and took his rather unwilling horse. Out of little more than curiosity, he did not head for the pass, instead making his way westward towards the canyon. He had a vague idea of finding a way across, but if he could not, it did not matter; he had lost nothing, time was simply the present as far as he was concerned.

TWO

It seemed that both the bartender and the sheriff knew what they were talking about; Brogan looked down a sheer drop of about four hundred feet, scanning the sides for any possible way down. In either direction, as far as he could see, the walls of the canyon offered no paths or footholds for a horse. Had he been on foot he had little doubt that he could have scaled the sides, but he was not on foot. He headed north for about half an hour, but there was still no sign of any way down or up, so he turned and headed south, towards the hills and the pass.

Two hours later – he had not hurried himself – he was looking at the point where the canyon began. The depth had dropped to about one hundred feet, but there was still no way down. In front of him the land started to rise quite steeply and, apart from heading into the pass, there did not seem to be any way round. He followed the rising ground towards the head of the pass when, although he could not see it, he knew there was a waterfall, his ears told him that much.

It took another half-hour to reach the waterfall and he looked at the river cascading over the edge

with some dismay. It was much too wide and
moving far too swiftly, making it very dangerous
to attempt a crossing so he had little choice but to
follow the river, reasoning that he must be able to
cross somewhere. Another half-hour and he still
had not been able to find a crossing place and, if
anything, the river was rougher and swifter than
before.

He had been following a definite trail for some
time and now he had little option but to continue
along it, the land either side, although not
impassable, was very steep and rock-strewn and,
since trails usually lead somewhere, it seemed
logical to continue along it, although his instincts
were against it.

Two minutes later he was aware of being
watched; he could not see anyone, but he knew
they were there. His hand automatically checked
his Colt in his holster and he continued to ride on.
He had had the feeling of being observed as he
had rode into the canyon that morning, but
nothing had happened so perhaps they would be
content to do nothing more than observe him
again – perhaps; he was ready, just in case.

The sense of being watched became stronger,
but by now he was passing through a narrow gully
with no means of escape. He smiled to himself; it
looked as if he was going to have to part with ten
dollars of his precious money, but that would be
better than trying to fight it out. In all he had
eighty dollars and a handful of small change –
seventy dollars would be more than enough for his
needs for quite some time.

'That's far enough!' a voice echoed somewhere

above him. He looked up to see a man holding a rifle steadily at him and knew better than even to attempt to go for his gun. For one reason, the man was out of the range of his Colt and for another he sensed that there were others not very far away and in any ensuing fight there could only be one loser – Brogan McNally! 'Figured you'd get round us,' boomed the voice again. 'Others've tried it but they didn't. They ought to've told you in town, we've got every way in an' out covered.'

'They told me!' called Brogan. 'Can't blame me for tryin' though, can you?' The man laughed, his laughter echoing round the hillsides. 'They also said it'd cost me ten dollars.'

'That's the normal charge,' another voice echoed somewhere in front of him but close at hand. 'OK, punk, ride on slow, real slow an' don't even think about goin' for your gun, there's eight rifles pointed at you right now.'

Brogan nodded and urged his horse slowly forward, following the trail between two large rocks and emerging to see five men ahead of him, all with rifles at the ready. Brogan looked around; the man who had stopped him was now behind him and two other men were perched on the top of each of the two large rocks.

'The dollars?' offered Brogan.

'You is the punk what came through this mornin',' grinned a big man, whom Brogan guessed to be Clem Cartwright; 'that makes it at least twenty dollars. Ten dollars is the normal charge for a horse an' rider, but that only applies to folk from Apache Falls. We got a sort of slidin' scale for strangers.'

'How much?' Brogan sighed, seeing even more of his precious money disappearing.

'Well now,' Cartwright grinned, 'that all depends on how much you got.'

'Supposin' I ain't got none?' said Brogan.

'Then we take what you have got,' replied Cartwright. 'We can always use guns an' ammunition or your boots an' clothes an' even horses.'

'You'd strip a man naked an' take his horse?' said Brogan.

'We ain't had to yet,' Cartwright nodded, 'but there's always a first time. OK, get off your horse – slow mind you – an' walk over here.' Brogan did as he was ordered and stood about two yards in front of Cartwright. 'Search him!' Cartwright ordered one of his men. 'I reckon that since you was prepared to pay ten dollars, you got more'n that.'

The man roughly searched Brogan, while another searched through his saddle-bags, but found nothing of interest. The man searching his body quickly discovered the eighty dollars and the small change, holding it out for Cartwright to see.

'OK, so I got more'n ten dollars,' sighed Brogan, knowing full well that they would take all of it.

'Eighty dollars!' Cartwright grinned. 'Ain't that some kinda coincidence; eighty dollars an' some change is just the toll charge.'

'You'd see a man with no money?' said Brogan.

'Oh, you won't be without money for long,' laughed Cartwright. 'You look like a saddlebum, smell like one too; you can do what we just done, steal it from somebody else. I reckon that's how you came by this in the first place, so it ain't really yours.' Brogan chose to ignore the comment.

'Nice Winchester!' said the man who had searched the saddle-bags. 'Better'n mine. I reckon the toll charge has just gone up again.' Cartwright simply smiled.

'Hell!' oathed Brogan. 'You gotta leave a man somethin'.'

'You still got your Colt,' said Cartwright. 'Think yourself lucky we don't take that too. OK, you can go on your way.'

Brogan remounted his horse, scowling at the man who had taken his Winchester, the face permanently etched in his memory. He turned to Cartwright, still glaring hatred. 'Tell me some-thin',' he said, 'how come you let me through before?'

Cartwright smiled. 'Two reasons: one, unless you tried the desert, there ain't no other way out an' two, you may be a saddletramp, but I know a gunfighter when I see one. There was only three of us watchin' you when you came through an' I don't reckon we could've taken you.'

'At least you know a better man when you see him,' sneered Brogan. 'You could've killed me easy enough though.'

'Maybe, maybe not,' said Cartwright. 'There didn't seem much point in tryin' since you had to come back. We could just as easy kill you now, ain't nobody gonna miss you that's for sure.'

'That's for sure,' agreed Brogan. He thought it wise not to provoke Cartwright further, just in case he did kill him, and urged his horse forward past the men and not looking back.

The narrow trail eventually came out on to the main trail through the pass and he continued his journey unhindered. However, he was still smarting at having been outwitted; it was not often that he found himself at a disadvantage and he did not like it.

'You ain't got some crazy notion of goin' back have you?' he asked himself.

'What's so crazy?' he replied. 'The bastards took all our money an' the Winchester.'

'It's crazy 'cos there's too many of 'em,' he said, 'an' 'cos you oughtta be thankful you got out of it alive.'

'Maybe so,' he muttered, 'but we gotta have some money an', more important, we gotta have that Winchester back.'

'Yeh,' he agreed with himself. 'Winchesters ain't easy to come by an' we sure couldn't afford to buy another one.'

'That's settled it then!' he decided.

As he continued his journey through the pass, he made a mental note of the layout of the land, how far he had travelled and, more importantly, the position of two outlaws posted near to the entrance of the pass. They made no attempt to stop him nor to hide their presence. An hour later he pulled up at a water-hole about three miles from the pass and considered his strategy.

He looked up at the sky; it would be dark in a couple of hours but he did not really fancy the idea of trying to locate them in the dark; dawn would be the best time, most men were not at their best at that hour. There was, of course, the problem of gaining access to the pass without being seen; the two guards had a clear view and anyone approaching could be seen quite easily from almost all directions. Somehow he had to get there without being seen.

He looked up at the sky again and smiled slightly; nightfall would provide the ideal opportunity; he could easily reach the pass, or very close to it, under the cover of darkness. He settled down for a few hours, satisfied with his decision.

It was two hours after sunset before Brogan made his move; he was in no hurry, quite certain that he would be able to find a suitable place to hide up until first light. Even so, he was cautious, his senses ever on the alert but, apart from the normal sounds of the night – which he was well used to – there was nothing.

The moon was just rising as he found himself within two hundred yards of the entrance to the pass and, remembering the lay of the land, he veered to his left and began the search for a suitable hiding place, one where he could leave his horse in safety, since it was his intention to go in on foot. Within ten minutes he had found the perfect spot, even down to a small pool of clear water. A brief survey of the land around him showed that he was well hidden and, satisfied, he settled down for the night. He would have liked a fire, days may have been hot, but nights were very cold, but he knew that it would be far too dangerous, so he had to content himself with huddling under his blanket, keeping warm as best he could. It was nothing new, he had had to do the same thing many times before.

* * *

The first light of daybreak saw Brogan quietly leaving his sanctuary although, as yet, being on the western side of the hills, everywhere was still firmly in the grip of deep shadows. He did not go directly into the pass, instead scaling the fairly steep side of the hill, leaving his horse safely hidden, which would bring him above the trail through the pass and the men keeping watch.

As he climbed it became easier to see what was around him and he made a note of various landmarks which would enable him to find his way back again. From a narrow ridge, he could see the two large rocks at the entrance to the pass where the two sentries had been posted and was not too surprised that he did not see anyone. The outlaws probably considered it unnecessary to keep a twenty-four hour watch.

His prime objective was to locate the outlaws' camp which, he reasoned, was probably not very far away from the spot where they had robbed him. He made his way cautiously along the rocky slopes, keeping a constant keen eye and ear for any sounds or movements.

He had travelled about half a mile when he suddenly hid behind a rock. The sound had been unmistakable; horses moving along the trail now about thirty yards below him. He waited and listened and eventually saw two riders slowly making their way along the trail towards the entrance. These were almost certainly the men who were to keep watch over the entrance and he allowed them to move on by, although he was tempted to take them out; it would have been quite easy, even with his Colt. He was doubly tempted when he recognized one of them as the man who had taken his Winchester.

Despite the desire to retrieve his rifle, he resisted the temptation; killing either or both of them at that moment would serve no useful purpose other than recovering his rifle and the shots were certain to be heard by the others and might well lead to problems that he could well do without at that moment.

He waited until they were well out of sight before moving on. Another sudden sound along the trail proved to be nothing more than a small herd of deer but, unlike the human travellers, they sensed his presence and turned back and disappeared the way they had come. Brogan did not really expect to see anyone else along the trail, but it was not a risk he was prepared to take so he kept to the higher ground.

The search for the outlaws' camp did not take very long, a tell-tale wisp of smoke soon indicated their position some half a mile ahead. He edged slowly towards the smoke, ensuring that he was well hidden, quickly and silently darting from rock to rock or bush to bush until he was within no more than one hundred yards. Still the only evidence he had was the column of smoke, drifting almost straight upwards in the windless morning.

His steady gaze swept the surrounding hills and land, his eyes and ears not missing a single movement or sound. He had half expected at least one lookout to be posted somewhere near the camp, but there was no sign of one. It seemed that

the outlaws were confident enough of the strength
of their position and their numbers for the
thought of surprise attack led to be a possibility.

Attack! With possibly twenty-three men still in
the camp, any form of attack was definitely out of
the question. Exactly what he intended to do
when he had embarked on this mission, he simply
did not know; that was usually Brogan's way, act
first and think later; it was very rare for him to
have a plan in mind. So far he had been lucky,
somehow he had always managed to defeat the
odds, but he did not feel over-confident this time,
not against so many men who, he knew, could
handle guns and would probably kill their own
mothers without giving it a second thought.

The trail was now about a hundred yards to his
right with the camp immediately in front of him
another hundred yards. In his mind's eye he was
weighing up the routes and opportunities for
escape, should such a course of action be found
necessary. Escape routes were always very
important; he had found that it paid handsome
dividends to weigh up all the possibilities
beforehand rather than act and then hope for a
way out.

He left his cover and slowly made his way to his
left to investigate the possibilities but very
quickly found himself looking down a sheer drop
of about two hundred feet. Any thought of escape
in that direction was very definitely out of the
question. On his side of the trail the only options
were along the trail itself or back along the high
ground the way he had come. There was, of
course, the other side of the trail and from where

he was it did not look too bad. He made his way towards the trail and hid between two large rocks and waited, sensing that something was going to happen. He did not have to wait very long.

There was the sudden sound of horses cantering along the trail and two riders appeared in front of him heading towards the entrance of the pass and he could hear more horses going in the opposite direction. How many were heading that way was difficult to tell exactly, but he guessed at least four. Two men on lookout at the beginning of the pass plus two more headed that way – for what purpose he had no idea but he did not think it was to relieve the two already there, it was too soon for that – and four heading the other way, that was eight men. The sheriff had confidently said twenty-five men and, if he was right, that left seventeen men unaccounted for – still not very favourable odds.

He waited for about five minutes before leaving his cover and racing across the trail to the safety of a thick clump of bushes. From there he cautiously made his way up the slope and over a ridge, coming out into a thickly wooded area. He smiled to himself, it was hardly likely that there would be any lookouts up here.

The swathe of woods was not very wide, only about two hundred yards and to his left it followed a narrow valley, sweeping southward. To his right the land rose steadily and he could see that the trees thinned out rapidly. He guessed that they stopped more or less at the high ridge overlooking the plain. Just how far the valley extended

southward he could not tell, but he was
reasonably certain that he would be able to leave
the hills that way if he needed to.

Satisfied, he made his way back to the trail,
crossed it and decided to take a look at the
outlaws' camp. Once again he checked for
lookouts but again there were no signs of any, so
he crept nearer the column of rising smoke.
Flattening himself on the ground under a bush, he
peered over the edge of a small hollow.

The camp appeared to consist of nothing more
than ten waterproof sheets spread across gaps
between the rocks. A fire burned in the centre of
the area and he counted twelve outlaws lying
about, including Cartwright. Twelve in camp,
eight on lookout, that still left possibly five men
unaccounted for. Two others were eventually
located tending the horses some ten or fifteen
yards away to his left, partly hidden by a large
bush. The whereabouts of the other three
remained unknown.

Cartwright was sitting on a metal box outside
one of the makeshift tents and Brogan guessed
that this box contained any money or valuables
they had, but any thought of trying to get the box
was out of the question. If he did start shooting he
could never hope to kill more than perhaps three
of them before they located him and then all his
time and effort would have been wasted.
However, he was quite determined to recover his
money and his rifle; he did not like the idea of
being robbed and outwitted.

'Damned stupid pride!' he muttered to himself.
'It'll be the death of you yet.'

'So I keeps on tellin' you,' he replied.

'Yeh, so you do,' he agreed. 'Don't make no difference though.'

'I know that, but just how the hell you gonna get it?'

'Dunno,' he muttered, 'but I will. OK, there ain't much point in stayin' here, there ain't nothin' we can do for now, let's go back an' think things over.'

'Yeh, let's go back,' he agreed with himself. 'Maybe we can forget all about it an' put it down to experience.'

'Yeh, maybe!' he sighed.

There was no difficulty in getting back, at least as far as the lookouts but here he was presented with the problem of crossing about fifty yards of loose scree which offered no form of cover whatsoever and in full view of the nearest lookout. For most of the time the man simply lounged, staring on to the plain in front of him, but every time Brogan was tempted to cross the scree it seemed the man turned his head in his direction. Brogan waited; he had all day.

There was no sign of the two men who had ridden out later and he was reasonably certain that they had not returned while he was surveying the upper valley and the woods. The question came to his mind 'Have they found my horse?' About half an hour later his question was answered when he saw them returning from the direction of the plain. Had they discovered his horse they would not be laughing and joking or travelling back at such a leisurely pace as they were now.

His opportunity to cross the scree came when

the lookout walked to the edge of his rock and called down to them. Brogan could not hear what was being said and he was not particularly interested as he made his move. Fortunately the two riders below could not see the scree, another few yards and they would have been able to; he just prayed that the lookout would keep them talking long enough for him to cross.

He was in luck, but only just; as he dived for the cover of a large rock on the other side, the two men appeared and their attention was attracted to the scree by the rattle of some loose stones which Brogan had dislodged. However, they did not stop, obviously assuming that it was just one of those things.

After giving them plenty of time to disappear, Brogan had no difficulty in reaching the safety of his hideout, where his horse looked at him as though he had just crawled from under a stone and continued her feed on the lush grass.

'It's all right for you,' grumbled Brogan. 'You can eat grass, I can't an' I'm starvin'. Since I don't reckon it'd be safe to light a fire, I guess I'll have to eat what bit of jerky I got. I don't like the stuff, but it's all I got 'ceptin' smoked bacon; don't fancy that either – not uncooked.' He opened his saddle-bag and took out a strip of leathery looking substance, eyed it dubiously, grunted and tore a piece off with his teeth. 'Ain't too bad if'n you swaller it I suppose!' he grumbled.

His jerky eaten, lying like lead on his stomach, his mind turned to other things, the prime one being how he was going to get his money and Winchester back. Eventually he smiled slightly.

He would go back to Apache Falls; he had a feeling that he would be able to enlist the help of the sheriff and possibly one or two others. He was going to need help; even he knew he could not hope to outwit the outlaws alone. Besides, the sheriff wanted to be rid of them as well.

'Kill two birds with one stone!' he grinned.

THREE

Brogan spent the remainder of the daylight hours sleeping, since there was not much else he could do; he could not chance going back to Apache Falls for fear of being seen. An hour after sunset he made his move, this time taking his horse with him, the prospect of which she seemed to resent. He rode past the entrance to the pass, reasonably secure in the knowledge that he would not be seen and, about half a mile further on, he turned up the steep, rocky slope of the hills.

It was not easy going; in daylight it would have been comparatively easy, but as there was, as yet, no moon, it was difficult to tell if the many black pools and shadows were rocks or holes. After a very short time he dismounted and led his horse, he felt it would be safer. Eventually he reached the top and could just make out the beginning of the trees some distance away.

The ground appeared fairly flat and even, free from rocks and sudden holes, so he mounted, urged his horse forward and allowed her to travel at her own pace. He was soon lost in the trees and even had there been moonlight, it would not have helped much. However, he knew that all he had to do was follow the forest, but he decided to keep as close to the edge of it as possible, looking out for various landmarks he had noted.

About an hour later he found a particular tall column of rock that he had been looking for and knew that he was well past the outlaws' camp. He left the shelter of the trees and rode towards the dark column, but from there on, he was in unknown territory, so he had to proceed with a certain amount of caution. By now the moon had risen, which helped him and, after about half an hour, he was looking down on to the plain, he guessed at about three miles south of the pass.

Descending on to the plain was a lot harder than it looked and twice he had to make detours to avoid sheer drops, but eventually he found himself safely on flat ground and heading north towards Apache Falls.

Rather to his surprise, there were still a few lights shining from some of the houses and the saloon appeared to be still open for business. He did not really expect to find many customers inside the saloon and he was right. He was greeted with amazed looks from the bartender and the three other customers, one of whom was the sheriff.

'What the hell you doin' back here?' demanded the sheriff.

'I come to talk to you,' replied Brogan. 'I got me a little problem.'

'Ain't we all got problems!' grumbled the bartender. 'So what's new?' Brogan ignored him and nodded to the sheriff to join him at a corner table. 'Drink?' prompted the bartender.

'No thanks,' replied Brogan, 'not unless you is givin' it away. That's my problem. I'm flat broke.'

'Broke?' queried the sheriff, joining him. 'How come?'

'Your friendly toll collectors took more'n ten dollars,' said Brogan. 'They took all I had, includin' about four dollars in small change. I had me more'n eighty dollars, now I got nothin'; they even took my Winchester.'

'Can't say as I'm surprised,' nodded the sheriff.

'I suppose I shouldn't be either,' grumbled Brogan.

'So what the hell you come back here for? I'd say you was invitin' even more trouble.'

'It's them what's askin' for trouble,' Brogan sighed. 'I don't take too kindly to bein' robbed.'

'Don't suppose there's any man what does,' smiled the sheriff. 'OK, since you is broke, I'll buy you a beer.' He nodded at the bartender who brought it over to the table. Brogan waited until the bartender had left them before speaking.

'Thanks,' he said. 'Another first! Must be about the first time any sheriff has bought me a drink, probably be the last too; most sheriffs is only too ready to run me out of their territory.'

'Maybe I oughta do just that,' nodded the sheriff. 'The name's Jarvis, Ben Jarvis.'

'McNally,' said Brogan. 'Brogan McNally, just call me Brogan.'

'OK, Brogan,' said Jarvis, 'so they took all your money an' your gun, so why the hell come back? I'd've thought you'd have more sense. Anyhow, just how the hell did you get back? That's twice you've got through without bein' stopped.'

'Seems they didn't fancy tacklin' me the first time,' said Brogan. 'But they'd got nothin' to lose, they knew I'd gotta go back. This time it was dark an' I didn't use the pass, climbed the hills an' followed a valley just south of the pass an' then cut down.'

'Sure,' nodded Jarvis. 'I've been that way myself a couple of times. It ain't too bad for a lone rider, but there ain't no way anyone can hope to get a wagon through.'

'So I found out,' agreed Brogan. 'I also found out exactly where their hideout is.'

'You've been that close to 'em without bein' seen?' Jarvis seemed very surprised.

'Yep, I been that close!' Brogan confirmed.

'Man, you gotta be crazy!' Jarvis shook his head. 'I got me this sickenin' feelin' you intend to go after 'em.'

'I don't like bein' robbed,' Brogan grinned. 'If they'd've settled for the ten dollars I wouldn't be here now, but they didn't, so I am. Only trouble is there's too many of 'em for me to handle on my own, I'm gonna need some help.'

'You're gonna need help!' muttered Jarvis. 'Mister, I been tryin' to get help ever since they've been up there, but I ain't got none yet. I ain't had no help from outside an' certainly no help from inside.'

'I'd say there was at least two willin' helpers,' reminded Brogan.

'Aaron an' Jake!' Jarvis laughed. 'Sure, but they're the only two an' I ain't too sure if they'd be a help or a hindrance. Their idea is to ride in cavalry style, guns blazin'.'

'I figured that might be the case,' grinned Brogan. 'They could be useful though. I know you're gonna think I've flipped my lid, but I reckon the two of us could take 'em. How about it?'

'Yeh, you've flipped your lid!' laughed Jarvis.

'Thing is,' smiled Brogan. 'You want rid of 'em an' I want my money an' my Winchester.'

'You know somethin',' smiled Jarvis. 'I do believe you're actually serious about it.'

'Oh, I'm serious,' assured Brogan. 'Never more serious. I ain't in the habit of sayin' things I don't mean.'

Jarvis studied his glass for a while before answering. 'I sure would like to be rid of 'em,' he said, 'but just the two of us? It ain't possible, not two against twenty-five.'

'Could even be more,' said Brogan.

Jarvis sighed heavily. 'Somethin's gotta be done, that's for sure, but two of us – maybe four with Aaron an' Jake – I dunno.'

'Tell you what,' offered Brogan, 'there sure as hell ain't nothin' we can do tonight so let's sleep on it an' we'll talk again in the mornin'. Right now I'm for gettin' my head down. Do you reckon you could square it for me to stay the night in the livery?'

'Shouldn't be no problem,' nodded Jarvis. 'He's my brother-in-law, I'll fix it.'

The blacksmith grumbled a little, but agreed to the sheriff's request and Brogan was able to settle down on some hay, his mind trying to recall the lay of the land around the outlaws' camp and thinking of ways to get to them. He did not think too long, soon drifting off into untroubled sleep.

* * *

'Are you hungry?' the sheriff asked as Brogan entered the office. 'I told my wife about you last night, about you havin' all your money took an' all that. Seems she felt kinda sorry for you, although I can't think why she should, an' she sent this over for you.' He pushed a plate of sandwiches across the desk.

'I guess I am kinda hungry at that,' Brogan grinned, 'although I still got my supplies. They never took them for some reason. I thank you kindly, Mrs Jarvis!' He took a large, appreciative bite of a sandwich, which proved to be cheese. 'Good cheese!' he said. 'Home-made?'

'Not by my wife,' said Jarvis. 'Mrs Wilkins, she's a real dab hand at makin' cheese an' butter. OK, I've thought about what you said an' I still think it's a crazy idea, but then this is a kinda crazy situation. I'm ready to listen, but I ain't promisin' nothin'. You had any more ideas?'

'Some,' mumbled Brogan through a mouthful of sandwich which he gulped and swallowed. 'Have you?'

'I've thought about nothin' else all night,' said Jarvis, 'an' for the life of me I can't see how it can be done, not even with four of us. If I could raise a posse or the army was to suddenly appear it'd be easier, but neither's likely to happen. Where Cartwright is holed up they could hold out forever.'

'A posse or the army would be too many men,' said Brogan. 'If they is expectin' anythin' they'll expect a lot of men. Two, or even four men can hide a whole lot easier'n a lot, move about easier an' keep 'em pinned down easier.'

'You make it sound like you is talkin' from experience,' Jarvis said.

'I am,' Brogan nodded, not attempting to explain any further. 'So what about Aaron an' Jake?'

'Thinkin' about it, I don't reckon Jake's gonna be much use, you made his gunhand pretty useless, remember.'

'So that leaves Aaron,' shrugged Brogan. 'Do you reckon he could be trusted to do as he was told?'

'Of the two, Aaron's the most likely,' said Jarvis, 'but we're talkin' as though I've already agreed to this crazy scheme of yours an' I ain't yet. Before I make any decision I wanna know what you got in mind.'

Brogan took another bite of his sandwich and chewed in silence for a while. 'Normally I don't make plans in advance,' he said eventually. 'I've always found they got this habit of goin' wrong.'

Jarvis laughed lightly. 'Me too. So we just ride up there, go in an' shoot 'em! That's a recipe for disaster if I ever heard one.'

'Could be the recipe for success,' said Brogan. 'That's just about the last thing they'll expect. The surprise alone might just sway things in our favour.'

'Glad you said "might just",' said Jarvis. 'In my book "might just" ain't good enough. Sorry, Brogan, you gotta come up with somethin' better'n that before I stick my neck out. I ain't scared, don't get the idea I am, I'm ready to die fightin' if

necessary, but I ain't ready to die when it ain't
necessary.'

'I never thought for one moment you was scared,'
assured Brogan. 'I reckon I'm a pretty good judge of
men an' I didn't have you down as no coward.'

'Thanks for that anyway,' grinned Jarvis. 'Why
should you bother though? I'd say you've been a
saddlebum all your life so you must have been in
the position of havin' no money before an' I'd say it
didn't bother you overmuch. I've seen a lot of
saddletramps an' drifters an' the only worry they
ever had was their own skins. If they needed
money they usually found some isolated homestead an' stole it.'

'Yeh, know what you mean,' Brogan sighed.
'Most saddletramps got a lot to answer for, they
give folk like me a bad reputation; but you can
believe this or not, I don't much care, I ain't never
in my life stole nothin' from nobody; I ain't never
murdered nobody; I ain't never raped a woman; I
ain't never cheated ...'

'An' you sure ain't no angel an' you never had a
bath!' Jarvis interrupted.

'Bathin', 'specially with real soap, ain't healthy!'
Brogan scowled. 'Just 'cos I don't smell too
wholesome don't make me no monster.'

'OK, OK,' laughed Jarvis, sensing that he had hit
a sore point, 'I believe you! What I don't believe is
that you ain't never killed nobody. I'm a pretty
good judge of men too an' I know you've killed, lots
of times I'd say.'

'I said I ain't never murdered nobody,' objected
Brogan, stiffly. 'I didn't say I'd never killed nobody.'

'OK, OK,' said Jarvis, 'somehow I kinda believe

you. As a matter of fact I've been lookin' through my files an' wanted posters to see if you was on one of 'em.'

'I ain't!'

'No, you're not,' agreed Jarvis, 'which makes you kinda special – special an' dangerous!'

'I'm only dangerous to them what deserves it or gets in my way,' said Brogan.

'Which makes you even more dangerous,' said Jarvis. 'You look like you could kill without givin' it a thought if you had to.'

'If I have to!' agreed Brogan.

'An' how are you about bein' killed, about dyin'?'

Brogan shrugged. 'I guess we all gotta die sometime.'

'It don't bother you?'

'It sure as hell won't bother me once I'm dead,' replied Brogan. 'No, I ain't scared of dyin'; can't say as I fancy the idea overmuch an' I'd hate to die before my time, but then how the hell does anyone know when their time is up, all it takes is one bullet? One second you is alive an' well an' the next ... Who knows what happens next?'

'There's plenty of preachers only too ready to tell you,' Jarvis laughed. 'Seems you got two options but no choice. You either end up up there, sproutin' wings an' learnin' how to fly, or down there stokin' up fires.'

'It must be kinda cold up there,' grinned Brogan, 'an' I don't reckon I'll ever learn to fly, so it looks like stokin' fires for me. That'll make a change, workin' after I'm dead. I sure as hell ain't never done none yet.'

'Then how in the hell d'you get your money? You

said you had eighty dollars.'

'That's what I had left from a little bit of bounty huntin',' said Brogan.

'Bounty huntin'?'

'Yeh. Don't get the idea that's how I earn my livin', it ain't. It just sorta happens that way sometimes, I kill a man what tries to kill me an' then find out there's a reward out on him. I ain't never gone outta my way to hunt a man though. Apart from that, I get by.'

Jarvis decided not to push the point. 'OK, I confess I'm interested in your idea, mainly 'cos of you; I reckon you could just pull it off. I ain't goin' in blind though, if you want to play it purely by ear then you're on your own.'

'I guess I can appreciate that,' said Brogan. 'You wanna bring in Aaron on these talks?'

'Not yet,' said Jarvis, firmly. 'If we think we'll need him I'll go get him. One of Aaron's problems is that he can't stop talkin' an' I don't want him blabbin' anythin' round town. He's spent most of his life in the cavalry, never got promoted as far as I know, said he didn't want the responsibility that went with it. He's used to takin' orders but not givin' 'em or actin' on his own.'

'Seems they did do somethin' on their own,' said Brogan, smiling and stroking his ear.

'That was Jake,' said Jarvis. 'Jake was a corporal, I think. To listen to him you'd think he'd been a general.'

'OK then, we'll leave 'em both out of it for the moment,' said Brogan. 'Have you got a map, one that shows the hills an' the pass?'

'I got one what shows the pass,' Jarvis grunted,

'nothin' much else though.'

'Then I guess it'll have to do,' said Brogan.

The sheriff rummaged through a drawer and eventually found what he was looking for, a faded map, and spread it across the desk. 'It's a few years old,' he apologized, 'but nothin's changed much.'

Brogan bent over the map and studied it while he ate another sandwich and eventually pointed to a spot about halfway along the pass, just off the trail. 'That's where they is hidin' out,' he said. 'But accordin' to the map there is only one way in an' out an' that's from the trail, but I know there's at least two other ways.'

'I said the map didn't show that much,' said Jarvis. 'For all I know there could be a hundred ways in an' out.'

Brogan grunted. 'This is the trail I went along, leadin' up from the canyon, accordin' to this it just disappears, but I know it don't. If we was to spook 'em they'd more'n like go down here. The only trouble with that is, an' they must know it too, there ain't nowhere's else to go.'

'Not only that,' said Jarvis, 'if they did go that way they'd more'n likely head for town; if they do that there ain't no way of knowin' just what they'll do. I do know that at least two of 'em ain't at all fussy 'bout who they kill, man, woman or child an' given the opportunity they'd rape every woman they came across.'

'Well unless we can do somethin' to stop 'em headin' that way,' said Brogan, 'that's a chance we'll just have to take.'

'I ain't in the business of takin' chances with

other folks' lives,' said Jarvis, very firmly. 'If, an'
only if, I agree to goin' along with you, we've gotta
make sure they never reach town or any of the
farmers.'

'OK,' Brogan sighed. 'I guess I'll have to go
along with that, although what the hell's to stop
'em doin' just that anyhow?'

'Cartwright!' said Jarvis. 'So far he's kept 'em
pretty well under control; he's even stopped 'em
rapin' women what've gone through the pass. He
ain't no fool, he knows that if his men so much as
lay a finger on any woman the whole town'll be
after him.'

'So why don't the whole town go after him
anyhow?'

'Simply 'cos he ain't done nothin' like that yet,'
said Jarvis. 'There ain't one of 'em prepared to
risk their lives just yet.'

Brogan sighed and shook his head. 'Yeh, folk is
like that. OK then, so we gotta block off his retreat
that way. Apart from havin' more men to hold him
back I reckon there's only one other way.'

'An' what's that?'

'Dynamite! I got me out of a few fixes with
dynamite before now.'

'I reckon we got plenty,' said Jarvis.

'Good,' said Brogan. 'I reckon we'll need it.' He
studied the map again, but eventually discarded
it because it showed so little detail. He would have
to rely on what he already knew and on what the
sheriff and Aaron or Jake might know. He had
long decided that he had to have another look at
the layout. 'Who knows this territory better'n
anyone else?' he asked. 'More 'specially, who

knows the hills an' the pass?'

'Pete Seagar; you've already met him, he runs the saloon,' replied Jarvis. 'An' the one person who knows more'n anyone is Mrs Grant, she's almost ninety but she was born here, long before Apache Falls ever existed as a town.'

'Might be a good idea if'n I talk to both of 'em,' said Brogan. 'The more I know about things the happier I am.'

'That ain't no problem,' said Jarvis. 'Who d'you wanna talk to first?'

'Since Mrs Grant was born an' raised here, I reckon she oughta know more'n most, let's go talk to her.'

FOUR

Sheriff Jarvis led Brogan up the street to a small, neat house, next door to the church. 'I don't know what she can tell you,' said Jarvis, 'or what use any of it'll be, but at least it shows you're methodical.'

'I don't know that either,' said Brogan, 'but it's worth a try. I like to have as much information as possible, even if I ain't got no use for most of it.'

Brogan was very surprised when Mrs Grant opened the door; somehow he had expected a small, wizened woman, but instead found himself face to face with a very tall, very thin woman whose looks belied her age. Sheriff Jarvis introduced Brogan and she looked at him with great suspicion.

'Saddlebum!' she sneered, with a lot of venom. 'What you wanna bring a saddlebum here for?'

'That's a long story, Mrs Grant,' said Jarvis. 'But puttin' it briefly, he's been robbed by Clem Cartwright – took all his money an' his rifle.'

'So what the hell am I supposed to do about it?' she rasped. 'The rifle must've been the only thing he had of value anyhow an' he probably stole it from someone else.'

Brogan sighed and smiled slightly, he was well used to such abuse, especially from women like Mrs Grant, who tended to think that he was about to rape them. 'Can we come in, Mrs Grant?' he asked, 'I need to talk with you.'

She sniffed the air, looked contemptuously at Brogan and quizzically at Jarvis. 'I keep a clean house,' she asserted. 'You wanna talk, you go round the back, there's a bench in the yard. What's all this about, young Jarvis?'

'Let's sit down an' we can explain,' said Jarvis. 'We'll go round the back.' He and Brogan ambled round to the back door, where Mrs Grant still refused to let them enter the house, pointing to a bench by the back door. She stood firmly on guard at the door while the two men sat down, waiting for someone to explain.

'You gonna start, Sheriff, or me?' said Brogan.

'I'd better explain,' said Jarvis. 'Mrs Grant, Mr McNally here seems to think that we might be able to get rid of Cartwright ...'

''Bout time somebody did!' she sneered. 'In my day they'd've been driven off or killed by now; we didn't stand around waitin' for someone else; we didn't have time; we had to do everythin' ourselves.'

'Maybe so,' agreed Brogan. 'I hear you've been in these parts all your life, so I guess you oughtta know the territory better'n anyone else.'

'Used to,' she snorted. 'Don't get about much these days, but I don't reckon things've changed all that much, 'ceptin' maybe a few more homesteads an' ranches, an' folk is more concerned about their own hides than they used to be. In the old days the farmers an' the ranchers would've banded together, had to when the Indians raided …'

'Yeh, sure,' said Brogan. 'I agree, most folk don't seem to care no more, even I noticed that. I reckon you're right when you say things ain't changed all that much. Apache Pass must be about the same too, what you know about it?'

'What's to know?' she replied, warming slightly to Brogan's smile. 'It's just about the only way in an' out of Apache Falls, unless you can cross the desert.'

'Do you reckon about twenty-five men holed up there could be flushed out?'

'Sure,' she laughed, 'why the hell not? In the old days we used to have problems with the Indians up there – don't think there's any left now – but we beat 'em. They used to reckon a whole army could hold out up there, but they can't have it all their own way, we simply sealed the Indians in an' then picked 'em off one by one or until they gave up.'

'That's one idea,' agreed Brogan. 'Only trouble with that is it's liable to take too long.'

'Took us about two months.'

'We got about two days!' said Brogan.

'Then I'd say you got more chance of bein' trampled by a herd of buffalo,' she laughed. 'An' there ain't no buffalo in these parts no more.'

'So you reckon there's nothin' you know which could help?' said Jarvis.

'Don't reckon so,' she replied.

'Well thanks anyhow, Mrs Grant,' said Jarvis. 'Sorry to trouble you.'

Mrs Grant was deep in thought. 'Is the dam still up there?'

'Dam,' queried Jarvis, 'what dam?'

'You don't know 'bout the dam?' she said. 'No, don't expect you do, you're a newcomer to these parts. Come to think of it I ain't heard about it myself for a long time.'

'I ain't exactly a newcomer,' objected Jarvis. 'I've been here more'n twenty years.'

'That's a newcomer as far as I'm concerned,' she laughed.

'Where abouts is this dam?' asked Brogan.

'In the early days, some sheep farmer named Thompson decided to build a dam. He wanted a lake so's he'd always have water for his sheep. I never actually saw it myself, but I heard it was built way up near the top of the hills; seemed a crazy place to put it, but then I guess that's where the sheep was. As far as I know it's still there.'

Brogan was suddenly very interested; he had not seen any sign of a dam or lake. 'Where exactly is this dam?' he urged.

'Don't know exactly,' she said. 'Told you, I never went up there, but I hear it was about half-way up the pass an' quite close to the trail; they used to reckon if it bust its sides it'd flood the pass. I seem to remember it bein' up on the left as you go through from this end.'

'You know about it?' Brogan asked the sheriff.

'I seem to remember somethin' about it,' replied Jarvis; 'didn't have no idea it'd been dammed up though.'

Brogan touched the brim of his hat and smiled at Mrs Grant. 'Thank you kindly, ma'am, could be a very useful bit of information.'

'Don't see how,' she countered, 'some folks is easy to please!' Brogan smiled again and once again touched the brim of his hat as he and the sheriff left.

'I must say I kinda agree with her,' said Jarvis. 'What use is the lake gonna be?'

'Right now I ain't got the faintest idea,' said Brogan, 'but I got me this sort of tinglin' feelin', which usually means I'm on to somethin'.'

'Unless you is gonna drown 'em, I don't see how it's gonna help,' said Jarvis.

'Me neither,' Brogan admitted. 'Let's go see Pete Seagar.'

Pete Seagar, owner of the saloon, confirmed the existence of the lake and the dam, although he was not old enough to remember it being built. 'From what I remember, the dam was built across what used to be a waterfall, nothin' spectacular they said, but it fell maybe a couple of hundred feet down into the river what runs by the trail. There's still plenty of water comes down the side of the hill when the lake's full an' overflows, but that usually only happens in the winter.'

'Mrs Grant said it was built by some sheep farmer,' said Brogan. 'Is there anyone still farmin' sheep up there?'

'No,' assured the sheriff. 'I did hear talk of a sheep farmer once, but that was a long time ago an' there ain't nobody up there now.'

'Then the lake's not been used by nobody,' said Brogan.

'So what?' shrugged Jarvis. 'Don't see how that helps.'

'Neither do I,' Brogan admitted, 'but I reckon I'll go take a look anyhow.'

'In daylight?'

'So, why not?' Brogan smiled. 'All I gotta do is get up there without bein' seen.'

'Easier said than done,' said Jarvis. 'Nobody knows where they keep their lookouts, chances are they'd spot you a mile off.'

'I'll figure somethin' out,' said Brogan.

'Maybe you won't have to,' said Pete Seagar. 'I don't know what you've got in mind an' whatever it is I reckon it's plain crazy, but Henry Ricketts has got to ride that way; says he's bringin' in some steers; he wants 'em nearer town.'

'So how does that help?' asked Brogan.

Seagar smiled slightly. 'I thought you was supposed to be able to look after yourself. Obvious ain't it? You ride out with Henry an' his men, like you was one of them. I doubt very much if they'd bother to count how many you are an' they sure as hell won't notice one missin' when the steers are driven back.'

Brogan laughed. 'I must be gettin' old! Sure, great idea, perfect cover. I shoulda cottoned on to it.'

'Henry should be here soon,' said Seagar. 'I don't suppose he'll mind if you use him as cover.'

'Thanks, I'll wait,' said Brogan. He did not have too long to wait; about ten minutes later a surprisingly small man entered the saloon, spoke briefly to Seagar and then turned and looked curiously at Brogan.

'I hear you got some crazy notion about gettin' rid of Cartwright,' he said as he walked over to

Brogan's table. 'Crazy or not, anythin' that'll get rid of him's gotta be good.'

'I ain't got no ideas in mind yet,' said Brogan, 'for the moment I'm just weighin' up the options.'

'So why should you bother?' asked Ricketts.

"Cos he took all my money an' my Winchester,' replied Brogan.

'That's all?'

'That's all,' Brogan nodded. 'If it was just your problem I don't reckon I'd bother.'

'Honest answer,' nodded Ricketts. 'So how can I help?'

'I hear you is ridin' out to round up some steers,' said Brogan. 'If I ride out with you, I can get close enough to the hills without bein' seen or at least noticed.'

Ricketts grunted. 'Don't know what you've got in mind an' I ain't gonna ask. Sure, you can ride out with us an' we'll take you as close to the pass or the hills as we can, but you're on your own, don't expect me or my boys to lift a finger to help you if you gets into trouble.'

'I won't,' assured Brogan.

There were four other men with Ricketts and after they were told why Brogan was joining them, they more or less ignored him, which did not worry Brogan unduly, but it was obvious that they were very curious about him, although they kept their curiosity to themselves and the ride south was taken in almost total silence.

They came to within about half a mile of the pass, but Brogan was unable to tell if they were being watched or not, so he waited until they were about a mile further on, when they were within about two hundred yards of the rising ground before he made his move. He nodded to Ricketts and rode quickly to the cover of some scrub.

After giving Ricketts and his men plenty of time to ride on and after carefully surveying the slopes above him, Brogan slowly made his way upwards, keeping a constant ear and eye open for any movements and eventually found himself amongst the thick woods off the valley he had followed. Exactly where the lake was nobody seemed to know, except that they were all agreed it was about half way and not too far from the outlaws' camp.

With that in mind, Brogan followed the line of the trees until he judged he was more or less on a level with their hideout. From this point he decided that it would probably be easier and safer if he continued on foot and hobbled his horse in a small clearing a few yards into the trees. He made a note of certain landmarks, drew a mental straight line from a tall, prominent rock and headed towards it.

Had he been seen, he had no doubts that they would have tackled him as soon as he reached the rock, but there was no challenge. His problem now was to locate the lake and, since directions had been so vague, it did not really seem to matter which direction he tried first. After half an hour of heading east, parallel with the trail, he decided to return to his starting point.

It only took another ten minutes searching in the opposite direction for him to find the lake, although it was not as big as he had expected, about fifty or sixty yards long and about twenty yards wide.

Alongside it were the remains of a rough home-stead, the stone walls still standing but the

timbers long since rotted away. A quick investiga-
tion revealed nothing of interest and he turned his
attention to the dam, the main reason for his
journey. It was obvious that it had been built
across a narrow gap between two mounds, each
only about twenty feet above water level and the
actual dam stretched about fifteen feet. He
assumed that the base of the dam was also the
depth of water on the other side and was
surprised that it was probably about twenty feet
deep, which indicated quite a volume of water
behind. He was also surprised at how well the
dam had been constructed.

A small stream entered the lake at the opposite
end and the level of water was close to the top of
the dam and seeped through some cracks to flow
some thirty yards before disappearing. He stood
at the edge of the drop and found himself looking
down on to the pass and he guessed, from certain
landmarks he recognized, that the outlaws' camp
was only about half a mile down the trail. Having
satisfied himself, he returned to the dam and
examined it more closely.

It certainly appeared to be very solidly
constructed, apparently consisting of rocks which
had been sealed with mud. There was no sign of
any water leaking through, only that near the top.
It was about ten feet wide at its base, widening
out at the top to about fifteen feet. He had to
assume that it would be quite a lot thicker at its
base than at the top, but even so, with
strategically placed dynamite, it would be quite
easy to blow it sufficiently for the pressure of
water behind to complete the job.

Already some sort of plan was forming in his mind, especially with the use of dynamite. He followed the ridge above the trail, noting the narrowest points and knew that, if necessary, he could easily block the trail, though since it was the only way in and out for the townsfolk, he did not want to do that. However, he did not feel that he had wasted his time; he liked to know of all the possibilities open to him.

Keeping well hidden, he studied the pass for quite some time. There was one lone rider heading up the pass and signs of activity at the outlaws' camp. After a time he decided that he had seen enough and made his way back, stopping briefly to examine the dam again and making mental calculations as to how much dynamite would be needed.

He collected his horse and eventually descended on to the plain, but there was no sign of Ricketts, although he would have been surprised if there had been. He slowly made his way into Apache Falls where he was met by a very curious sheriff.

'Find the lake?'

'Large pond!' Brogan laughed, dismounting and tethering his horse. 'It's got good possibilities though.'

'Had any more thoughts on what to do?'

'Some,' admitted Brogan. 'How much dynamite can you raise?'

'Some!' smiled Jarvis. 'I reckon I can lay my hands on maybe fifty sticks if need be.'

'Should be more'n enough,' Brogan nodded. 'Let's have a look at that useless map of yours.' Jarvis nodded and led the way into his office where he produced the map. Brogan studied it for some time before resting his finger on a spot just off the trail. 'That's where it is.'

'That close to the trail?' said Jarvis.

'That close,' nodded Brogan. 'I'm kinda surprised nobody seems to know where it is.'

'Most folks never had cause to go up there,' said Jarvis. 'I know I've never been up there an' I've been here more'n twenty years.'

Brogan shrugged. 'Still find it kinda strange.' He picked up a pencil and drew the rough shape of the lake, making a point of showing the dam and the gully to the edge of the pass; he also marked the position of the outlaws' camp.

'You quite certain about where they is holed up?' asked Jarvis.

'As sure as I can be,' replied Brogan. 'An' more sure than most seem to be about the lake.'

Jarvis laughed. 'OK, I'll take your word for it. While you was away I had a word with the mayor, Andrew Travers, an' I've gotta tell you he ain't at all keen on you interferin' in our affairs.'

'Then you go right back an' tell him I ain't the slightest bit interested in what happens to this town; if I hadn't lost my money an' Winchester, I'd've been long since clear of here an' your problems. All I'm interested in is myself.'

Jarvis laughed. 'I already told him that. To put it mildly he told me to run you outa town before you caused trouble.'

'An' are you?'

'I'm thinkin' about it. Could be he's right at that, but I've told him I'm prepared to listen to what you've got in mind. Travers ain't such a bad guy; he wants to be rid of Cartwright just as much as anyone else.'

'An' like everyone else he ain't prepared to do a damn thing about it himself,' Brogan smiled.

'Maybe so,' agreed Jarvis, 'but I reckon he'll back anyone what does, if he thinks it'll work. OK, so you've been up there an' seen the layout, has it given you any ideas?'

'I'm still workin' on it,' replied Brogan. 'It ain't gonna be easy, but I reckon it can be done, even if there is only two of us.'

'It could be that you is on your own,' said Jarvis.

'In which case I cause as much havoc as I can an' they'll blame you. I take what I can lay my hands on an' get the hell out of it. One thing's for certain, I ain't gonna stick my neck out to help you or anyone else what don't want no help.'

'I ain't said nothin' about not helpin',' said Jarvis. 'Up to now I've been a lone voice an', like you, I had almost come to the point of givin' up. Sure, I wanted to be rid of Cartwright, but I'm not prepared to ride up there on some hare-brained scheme that's pure madness.'

'OK,' sighed Brogan, 'I guess I can accept that. For the moment I gotta assume that there's only you an' me. First we gotta create a diversion some-where's near this end of the pass – a couple of sticks of dynamite should do that easy enough, maybe we can block the pass or somethin'. Then, when they all ride out to see what the hell's goin' on, we close in behind them an' pick 'em off one by one.'

'Sounds too easy,' said Jarvis.

Brogan smiled and shook his head. 'Why is it that everybody is always lookin' for somethin' more complicated? Most folk seem to have the idea that 'cos somethin' is simple it ain't gonna work. It's 'cos it's simple that it could work.'

'OK,' agreed Jarvis, 'maybe it could work. Just supposin' Cartwright don't bite though an' he sits tight, what do we do then?'

'Then we gotta have some kinda back-up plan,' said Brogan.

'Such as?'

Brogan shrugged. 'I ain't figured that out yet, personally I don't reckon we'll need it. Anyhow, why is it me what has to put forward all the ideas? You musta given it some thought; you sure had time enough.'

'Sure, I had the time,' agreed Jarvis. 'We all had plenty of that, but either nobody wants to know or they can't come up with any ideas, me included.'

'Well apart from gettin' everybody together an' runnin' 'em out, it looks like any ideas I got are the only choices you got.'

'I'll still have to think about it,' said Jarvis. 'One thing we have got is time.' Brogan could only agree with that; time was certainly one commodity he had an abundance of.

'I can't hang about for ever though,' said Brogan.

Jarvis was looking at the map. 'I agree we gotta create some sort of diversion, but it'd be better if you an' me was to come at 'em from the canyon side, maybe Aaron or Jake could create the diversion.'

'Now you is beginnin' to think,' smiled Brogan. 'Only trouble with that idea is that they'll have us spotted long before we can reach 'em an' long before anyone can create a diversion, but don't let it bother you, you keep right on thinkin'!'

Jarvis smiled and indicated that he wanted to close his office and Brogan took the hint and left. Since he had no money there seemed little point in going into the saloon, nor could he put his horse in the livery, the blacksmith had made it plain that one free night was all he was prepared to stand, so he decided to go down to the river, where he could at least cook himself a meal and his horse would have water and good grazing.

Down by the river, Brogan found that he was not alone, a rather scruffy, elderly figure had his back towards him. The man eventually turned and proved to be Aaron. 'I heard you was back in town,' he muttered. 'Jarvis reckons you got some idea about gettin' rid of Cartwright.'

'Could be,' nodded Brogan, turning his horse loose. 'From what he told me, you had some ideas as well.'

'Too old!' muttered Aaron. 'That's my problem, leastways Jarvis reckons I'm too old. Maybe he's right, I dunno. Time was when I could've run 'em out single-handed.'

'Do you reckon you can still use a gun?' said Brogan. 'I don't mean fast, I mean straight.'

'You got a scar on your ear what says I can,' said Aaron.

'That's what I mean.' Brogan smiled. 'I shoulda been dead; you don't get too many shots at an easy target like I was.'

'Yeh, OK,' mumbled Aaron, 'point taken. Don't it bother you none that I might've killed you?'

'Nope!' laughed Brogan. "Cos if'n you had, I sure

wouldn't be bothered would I, I'd've been past carin'!'

Aaron shook his head. 'Yeh, I guess you're right about that. Sure, I reckon I can shoot as straight as most, better'n a good many; I've been trained by the military. I also got the advantage that I can shoot a man an' not think about it. You'd be surprised how many folk freeze up when they got a man in their sights.'

'No I wouldn't,' assured Brogan. 'It could be I could use you. Sure, I got a few ideas spinnin' round in my head, but I ain't so much interested in this town as gettin' my money an' Winchester back.'

Aaron looked quite pleased. 'You reckon you could use me? You just say the word an' I'll prove to this town that Old Aaron's got more guts than all of 'em put together.'

'You'll have to take orders an' follow 'em,' warned Brogan. 'If I do decide to go ahead it's gotta be a team job, no mavericks, can't afford 'em.'

'I was cavalry, remember!' smiled Aaron, toothily.

'I'll think about it an' let you know,' promised Brogan.

FIVE

Brogan saw nothing more of Sheriff Jarvis for the remainder of the day and he was in no particular hurry to get things moving. He spent that night under the shelter of a large, overhanging rock down by the river. The following morning he was up and about just before dawn. He seemed to be alone; the town of Apache Falls, it seemed, did not come to life until after sun-up.

The first signs of life came from the general store as the storekeeper noisily removed the shutters and began to lay out his wares. A few other residents slowly began to appear and eventually Sheriff Jarvis ambled towards his office. Brogan too slowly made his way to meet the sheriff.

'Had any more thoughts?' Brogan asked.

'I've thought of nothin' else,' replied Jarvis. 'I had a long talk with the mayor an' I think we're both agreed, it's no-go; it's far too risky.'

Brogan was not too surprised, although he was very disappointed. He shrugged. 'That's it then!'

'That's it,' said Jarvis. 'Sorry, I like the idea, an' all of us would like to see the end of Cartwright, but I agree with the mayor, there're too many of

67

them an' too many things could go wrong.'

'So I kiss my Winchester an' eighty dollars goodbye.'

'Afraid so,' agreed Jarvis. 'I hope you get past 'em.'

'Gettin' past 'em ain't no problem at all,' said Brogan. 'It wouldn't've been no problem before if somebody'd told me about it.' He returned to saddle his horse, feeling very aggrieved, although he could well understand the reluctance. He briefly toyed with his threat to create mayhem in the Cartwright camp, but decided that was being churlish. He was riding slowly past the sheriff's office when Old Aaron raced breathlessly into town, falling off his horse outside the office.

'Sheriff! Sheriff!' he gasped as Jarvis came out to see what all the commotion was about. 'They're comin'!'

'Who's comin'?' demanded Jarvis.

'The outlaws!' pouted Aaron. 'They're comin'!'

'All of 'em?' Jarvis demanded again.

'No!' gasped Aaron, flopping on to the boardwalk. 'Four of 'em!'

'You sure it's them?' asked Brogan.

'It's happened before,' said Jarvis. 'My guess is they need some supplies.'

'You mean you just let 'em ride in an' out when they want to?'

'They don't come in that often,' said Jarvis.

'So why don't you arrest 'em?'

'What's the point?' Jarvis shrugged. 'The others'd simply ride in an' get 'em out an' the Lord only knows what damage they'd do.'

'Shoot 'em!' grated Aaron, now recovered from

his exertions.

'That's your answer to everythin',' said Jarvis. 'That wouldn't solve nothin'.'

'Shoot 'em!' repeated Aaron.

Sheriff Jarvis sighed and bent down to relieve Aaron of his guns. 'Just in case!' he said. 'The old goat's just liable to do somethin' stupid like that.'

Brogan decided to wait around, not with any particular idea in mind, more an idle curiosity as to the reaction of the townsfolk. As things turned out, there were very quickly no townsfolk around to see how they reacted. As soon as word spread that the four outlaws were heading for town, they all disappeared, leaving Brogan, Old Aaron and Sheriff Jarvis and the owners of the three stores – general store, corn seed store and the hardware store – to face them.

It was about twenty minutes before they appeared, obviously in no great hurry, and they ignored the three men outside the sheriff's office, going straight for the general store. When they eventually emerged with various items, they called to the storekeeper to 'Put it on the bill!' and laughed loudly. Their next stop was the hardware store.

Brogan had suddenly become very interested. One of the outlaws was the one who had taken his Winchester, which Brogan could see was now resting in the man's saddle-holster. Sheriff Jarvis tried to grab his arm as Brogan walked past, but the hand was simply shaken away and he ambled towards the four horses. They were still in the hardware store as Brogan reached up and drew his Winchester from the holster.

'An' just what the hell d'you think you're playin' at?' a voice roared from the doorway of the hardware store. The man's actions were severely limited by arms full of goods.

'Retrievin' my property,' said Brogan, levelling the Winchester at the man's chest. The outlaw simply stood petrified. 'Wasn't very nice of you to take my gun,' continued Brogan.

'You ... you're the guy what came ...'

'The same,' agreed Brogan. The man was joined by the other three who could do nothing more than stand and stare.

'How the hell did you get back here?' the man gulped.

'It don't matter none how I got here,' replied Brogan, 'thing is, I don't like bein' robbed. I got my rifle back so all I need now is my eighty dollars, so you just hand it over an' I'll be on my way.'

'Eighty dollars!' growled one of the others. 'We ain't got eight between us.'

'Pity,' Brogan sighed. 'Still, I got my Winchester back. Tell me somethin', if you ain't got that much money, how the hell you gonna pay for all the things you got?'

'Pay!' the second man sneered. 'We don't pay for nothin'!'

'A man could go broke very quick if everyone thought like that,' said Brogan, 'an' if that happened, the likes of you'd have nobody to steal from. I'd say it'd be only right if you didn't take things if you ain't got the money to pay for 'em.'

The four outlaws were at an obvious disadvantage and looked helplessly at each other. 'Guess you got the drop on us,' muttered one, depositing his armful of goods on to the boardwalk; the others followed suit.

'An' now all the things you took from the general store!' ordered Brogan. They looked at each other again and shrugged and unloaded their horses, again depositing the goods on the boardwalk. Brogan stepped back slightly and allowed them to mount their horses.

'You is gonna be sorry for this!' threatened one.

'Maybe,' Brogan nodded, 'but I don't like bein' robbed an' it ain't right for you to take them things without payin' for 'em. Now, on your way while you can.'

The four men cast surly, threatening looks at the saddletramp who had had the nerve to confront them and, suddenly, the one nearest Brogan swung his horse broadside on and at the same time one of the others swung his horse in the opposite direction. Three shots echoed off the surrounding buildings; four horses reared and neighed in alarm and three bodies thudded to the ground. The fourth outlaw steadied his horse and looked at Brogan, sheer terror clearly showing in his eyes. He alone had not gone for his gun. Quite suddenly he spurred his horse into action and raced out of town, fully expecting to feel a bullet in his back. For a moment, Brogan was tempted, but lowered his Winchester and allowed the man to escape. There was pandemonium in Apache Falls; people suddenly appeared as if by magic, all keeping a respectful distance from the saddletramp.

'Christ!' muttered Sheriff Jarvis, bending down to examine the bodies. 'Won't be no need to go after 'em now, they'll come here!'

'Could be,' agreed Brogan. 'You'd better be ready for 'em.'

A man whom Brogan took to be the mayor, Andrew Travers, pushed his way through the crowd and stood in horror, glaring first at Brogan and then at the sheriff. 'I told you to get rid of this madman!' he shouted at Jarvis. 'Just look what the hell he's gone an' done now!'

'I was just leavin' when they rode in,' said Brogan, calmly.

'So what the hell you want to shoot 'em for?' demanded Travers.

'I didn't plan it.' Brogan shrugged. 'Just the way things turned out. One of 'em, the one what got away, was the one who stole my Winchester ...' he raised the rifle slightly – 'I was just recoverin' my property.'

'All dead!' pronounced Sheriff Jarvis. 'I seen some pretty fancy shootin' in my time, but I only counted three shots.'

'Three was all that was needed,' said Brogan, a little smugly. 'I don't believe in wastin' bullets.'

'Yeh, an' I don't reckon they was just lucky shots either.'

'It don't matter if they was lucky shots or not,' scowled Travers. 'The point is they're dead an' that's all that matters an' I don't think Cartwright is just gonna sit up there an' do nothin'.'

'Like I said,' grinned Brogan, 'maybe you'd better be ready for 'em. I reckon you got Cartwright outnumbered by at least ten to one, so you shouldn't have no problems.'

'An' just what the hell are you gonna do now?' demanded Travers.

'Be on my way, I reckon.' Brogan laughed. 'That's what you wanted, ain't it?'

'Typical saddletramp!' muttered Travers. 'Run out as soon as there's possible trouble!'

That remark had the effect of annoying Brogan. 'I didn't notice you or anyone else in this town try an' stand up to 'em just now!' he hissed. 'You was all too busy hidin' your butts! Mr Mayor, or whatever you is, there ain't nobody got cause to call me. There was four of them an' only one of me! There's well over two hundred people in this town an' only about twenty-five of them – three less now – an' you, none of you, 'ceptin' maybe Sheriff Jarvis, Jake an' Old Aaron, got the guts to stand up to 'em! I even offered to help but you didn't wanna know, too scared it might just go wrong an' you'd end up holdin' the sticky end. Takin' all that into account, I kinda resent someone like you accusin' me of runnin' scared.'

Mayor Travers looked very sheepish and glanced nervously at the crowd surrounding him. 'Yeh, well, sorry,' he muttered. 'I didn't mean to say you was a coward, but we wouldn't have this problem if you hadn't come back.'

'Wrong, Mr Mayor,' grated Brogan. 'You'd still be here an' Cartwright'd still be sittin' out there an' three storekeepers would be poorer. The only difference my comin' back has made is to possibly make you take some action.'

'It's the best thing that could've happened!' shouted Aaron. 'Jake an' me been tellin' you all along you gotta do somethin', but you just said we was a couple of old fools. Maybe now we'll see who the fools are!'

Sheriff Jarvis nodded to Brogan to follow him to his office, leaving Mayor Travers to organize the removal of the bodies and their horses.

'I don't know for sure,' said Jarvis as Brogan closed the door, 'but maybe what you did was a good thing – maybe – at least now we know we gotta do somethin'. Travers was right when he said Cartwright won't just sit back an' do nothin'. Is your offer still open?'

'I don't reckon you is gonna need it,' said Brogan. 'There's more'n enough of you.'

'I ain't too sure about that,' mused Jarvis. 'I'd like to think I'd got someone on my side what knows what they're doin'.'

'Accordin' to your mayor, I don't know what I'm doin'.'

Jarvis shrugged. 'It ain't gonna be him what has to face up to Cartwright.'

'I'll think about it,' said Brogan.

Clem Cartwright looked scornfully at the man standing in front of him attempting to explain what had gone wrong. 'You mean to tell me that four of you couldn't take one man! I thought any one of you could take any man you came up against, leastways that's the way you always told it.'

'He had the drop on us,' grumbled the man.

'Seems any kid could've got the drop on you,' sneered Cartwright. 'What's happened to them? You don't know if they is dead or not, do you? You was too busy savin' your own skin.'

'That's no more than you or any other man here would've done,' replied the man, defiantly.

Cartwright grunted. 'Yeh, maybe so, but I still don't understand how the hell you managed to let one man get the better of you. OK, so it's happened; there ain't nothin' we can do about it now. What we gotta think about is gettin' this stranger an' teachin' the folk of Apache Falls they can't mess about with us.'

'That shouldn't present no problems!' laughed one of the others. 'We just ride in, kill this saddlebum an' maybe a few of the others.'

Cartwright gave a deep sigh and looked scornful. 'So we just ride in an' kill him! I suppose you reckon they is just gonna stand around and watch us do it. I don't suppose it's occurred to you that this saddlebum might just fight back, an' maybe one or two others? Don't you think that's just what they'll expect us to do, or at least not be surprised if we do? I suppose the possibility that they may even fight hasn't crossed your mind?'

'The saddlebum sure seems to be able to handle himself,' said the first man, 'an' he sure don't seem scared.'

'We made a mistake in lettin' him live,' said Cartwright. 'I thought about it at the time. He struck me then as a man not to be messed around with. Still, we didn't kill him. OK, I'll have to think about it. In the meantime, make sure that all possible ways out are covered, just in case he does try to leave.'

Four extra men were despatched to the end of the pass, two more to the far end and three up to the top of the pass, overlooking the forest. Cartwright seemed satisfied that all possible exits were covered and sat down to consider his next move.

Unlike practically everyone else in Apache Falls, neither Brogan nor Sheriff Jarvis really expected Cartwright and his men to be foolish enough to simply ride in, but both knew that he would not stand aside as if nothing had happened. For some reason known only to himself, Brogan felt beholden to remain and see what he could do to help, although Mayor Travers was still not very keen on the idea.

'I've got me this feelin' that Cartwright'll try takin' it out on some of the outlyin' farms,' said Jarvis.

'Maybe they'd better be warned,' suggested Brogan, 'an' maybe a few men sent out to guard 'em.'

'Fine idea,' agreed Jarvis, 'but there're just two problems. One, there're three likely targets an' two, who the hell is there to send out? Apart from you, me an' Old Aaron, I can't see anyone else bein' prepared to risk their lives. Assumin' one of the farms is gonna be attacked, that means one of us at each, not exactly enough to repel upwards of twenty men.'

'Don't folk round here care about what happens to their neighbours?' asked Brogan.

'All most of 'em care about is their own skins,' Jarvis sighed. 'Sure, they is all full of grand talk about lookin' after each other, but there're so many petty feuds goin' on that each'd be hopin' his neighbour would be the one to get killed. Oh yeh, I'm sure they'd fight if the town was attacked, but that's the only time. Their philosophy is that the farmers gotta look after themselves.'

'So we got the three of us,' mused Brogan, shrugging. 'I been up against worse odds, but I could rely on a bit of help from somewheres else. Thing is, even three extra guns out at the right farm could make 'em think again. Where are these three farms?'

'I'll show you on the map,' said Jarvis.

The three farms formed a semi-circle around the entrance to the pass, all roughly the same size, although the farm furthest north, nearest Apache Falls, had its buildings nearer the pass than the others. The river separated the farm farthest south from the others and Brogan was inclined to think that this most southerly farm would be the most likely target.

'How many folk live here?' Brogan indicated the farm.

'The Westons,' said Jarvis. 'Jim Weston, May, his wife, one boy aged about seventeen, I think, another boy aged about fourteen an' three daughters, nine, thirteen an' sixteen.'

'The seventeen-year-old is another gun,' said Brogan, 'an' most farmers can shoot pretty good when they have to. Maybe the fourteen-year-old along with the eldest girl can shoot too.'

'I wouldn't count on it,' said Jarvis. 'The fourteen-year-old boy may want to, but his pa might not let him an' I'm damned sure he ain't gonna risk his girls.'

'Probably you is right,' sighed Brogan. 'It could be that Cartwright'll leave the farmers alone, but I guess we gotta assume he is gonna do somethin' an' it's gonna be against one of these three farms

an' I got me this feelin' that he'll choose the
Weston place.'

'What makes you think that? Campbell's place
is nearer the pass.'

'Just 'cos the Weston place is furthest away,'
said Brogan. 'Cartwright is liable to figure that we
is expectin' him to do somethin', but he'll reason
we'll think he's gonna hit the Campbell place, so
he'll hit the Westons. If I'm right an' you, me an'
possibly Aaron go there, that'll give us maybe six
guns; that oughta be enough, 'specially if they
ain't expectin' nothin'.'

'OK,' agreed Jarvis, 'I'll go along with that. I
reckon we've got to do somethin' an' I only hope
you is right an' they do try somethin' on the
Weston farm; we're gonna look pretty stupid if
they don't.'

'Then we'd better go now,' said Brogan. 'There's
no knowin' when Cartwright is gonna make his
move; let's just hope he ain't had time to yet. You
go get Aaron, I know he's old but he can shoot an'
he ain't scared.'

Clem Cartwright had given a lot of thought to
retaliation and his next move. At the very least he
was determined that someone had to be taught a
lesson, but at the moment he was not prepared to
take the risk of attacking Apache Falls. From his
vantage point high above the trail at the end of
the pass, he could see quite plainly the buildings
of the nearest farm and could just make out the
Weston farm to the far side. He toyed with the idea
of burning out the Campbell farm but decided
that it was too close to town and the townsfolk

might just be riding out to protect it, so he settled on the Weston farm.

'Burn 'em out!' he muttered. 'Burn 'em out an' make 'em hand over the saddletramp. If they don't hand him over I'll burn out one of the others.' He clambered down the hillside back to the trail and summoned eight of his men to follow him. Eight men were more than enough to deal with one small farm consisting of one man, one woman and one boy – the other children he discounted entirely.

'They got a pretty daughter,' grinned one of the men. 'Mrs Weston ain't such a bad looker either.'

'I don't want any of that!' warned Cartwright. 'Not this time anyhow. All we is gonna do is burn 'em out.'

'You gonna try an' stop any of us takin' the woman or the girl?' challenged the man.

'If I have to!' grated Cartwright.

'We'll see!' The man grinned, followed by large grins from the others and a wetting of lips in anticipation.

SIX

Brogan insisted that they must go to the Weston farm by following the course of the river, his argument being that the direct route across the plain offered no cover at all and their approach would be easily seen by anyone. Although following the river added perhaps another three miles to their journey, it did keep them fairly well concealed, at least until they were within about a quarter of a mile of the Weston farm.

If Jim Weston were at all upset or annoyed at the news, he did not show it, in fact almost welcoming the fact that someone had at last done something. At first he refused to believe that they would attack his farm, but he could see the reason behind Brogan's argument.

'It might not happen,' said Jarvis, 'but just in case it does, I'd send the girls an' the youngest boy into town.'

'Makes good sense,' agreed Weston, 'an' I'll send May as well, but young Jamie is handy with a rifle, even if he is only just fourteen.' The news pleased Jamie but not his mother, who tried to insist on him going and her remaining, but Jim Weston was adamant and, rather grudgingly,

81

May Weston loaded the girls on to a wagon and drove out, again following the river, for Apache Falls.

'How soon you expectin' somethin' to happen?' asked Jim Weston. 'Always supposin' you're right an' Cartwright does pick on my place, which don't really make a whole lotta sense.'

'There ain't no way of tellin',' said Brogan; 'they could be here any time now. I suggest you all go take up your positions in the house. I'm goin' up in the barn; I oughta be able to see 'em comin' from up there an' it could be that at least one of 'em'll head straight for the barn to set fire to it. You boys …' – he addressed Jamie and his elder brother – 'don't get no fancy ideas. You do exactly what you is told to do. You understand?'

'Yes, sir,' replied Jamie, proudly, his fingers running up and down the stock of his rather ancient rifle, in anticipation. 'I can shoot as straight as anyone else. I've won me a couple of prizes at the fair last spring.'

'Target shootin' ain't the same thing as bein' able to squeeze that trigger when you've got a man in your sights an' knowin' that you is liable to kill him.'

'I know that, sir,' said Jamie, 'but I killed me a few deer an' rabbits an' three coyotes, so a movin' target ain't no problem.'

'Deer an' coyotes ain't the same as human bein's,' reminded Brogan. 'I ain't never yet heard of no deer or coyote shootin' back.'

'Jamie'll be all right,' assured his father. 'I'll keep him alongside me. Carl won't be no problem.' Carl was the elder boy.

'You reckon you could shoot a man?' Brogan asked Carl.

'Don't want to,' replied Carl, 'an' I ain't never had to, but reckon I can.'

'OK,' Brogan nodded. 'Now we don't know for sure if they'll come; it could be that I figured things completely wrong an' they'll pick on one of your neighbours – I sure hope not. I've been wrong before, but I don't think me bein' wrong has been liable to mean someone else gettin' killed. Another thing we don't know is just how many of 'em'll come. Personally I can't see all of 'em comin'; it won't need that many to deal with one farm. Whatever happens I don't reckon we're gonna solve any problems, in fact it could even make 'em worse.'

'I for one am ready to take that chance!' assured Jim Weston. His eldest son nodded in agreement.

'Me too,' nodded Jarvis.

'I allus said we should've done somethin' like this ages ago!' snorted Aaron. 'It's a pity you had to shoot up Jake's gun hand; he's pig-sick at not bein' here.'

'It could be he'll still get some action,' said Brogan. 'OK take up your positions; I'm goin' up in the barn. I'll let you know as soon as I see somethin'.' He ran across the yard and climbed up into the roof of the barn, looking out of a loading door which gave him a good view in most directions except due east, but he was not too worried about the possibility of them coming in from the east.

Brogan smiled with a certain amount of self-satisfaction as the first signs of riders approaching came about twenty minutes later in the form of a cloud of dust, about two miles away. He called down to Aaron who was waiting at the back door of the house and he in turn relayed the information to the others. Sheriff Jarvis actually felt relieved that the choice of farm had been correct. It would have been little consolation to either Jim Weston or the other farmer had they got it wrong.

Brogan had also given instructions to those inside not to open fire as soon as the outlaws were in range. There were two reasons for this; one, he had to be quite certain that the first to arrive were the only ones, and two, he did not want them scared off too soon.

The dust cloud drew nearer and, when they were about a hundred yards away, they slowed down to a slow walk. Brogan could see that the lead horse was ridden by Clem Cartwright and he counted eight other riders. His keen eyes probed the plain behind them for signs of others, but he was satisfied these men were the only ones. They approached to within about twenty yards of the house, making Brogan curse slightly since his view of them was blocked by the house, but he heard Cartwright call out.

'You in there, you got two minutes to get your wife an' kids outa there; after that we burn it down whether you is out or not!'

Once again Brogan cursed as Cartwright's instructions were answered by a shot from the house. In the ensuing confusion, he was unable to tell if anyone had been hit or not. The fact that there were no loose horses indicated that none of the outlaws had been killed or injured. It was obvious that the outlaws were taking cover behind whatever they could and all except one were out of Brogan's sight.

However, the man in Brogan's sights was given a temporary reprieve as another outlaw came darting from behind a shed carrying a lighted pitch-torch. At first Brogan thought he was going to throw it on to the roof of the house, but suddenly the man was dashing across the yard towards the barn.

The man only managed to make it about halfway across the yard before he was felled by a single bullet from Brogan's Winchester. The torch, however, shot from the man's hand as he fell and spun across the dry earth, coming to rest just outside the barn door which was liberally strewn with dry hay and straw. Very rapidly the flames spread across the floor towards the main piles of hay and straw.

Brogan hesitated, glancing down at the spreading flames, but he raised his rifle at the one other outlaw he had clear sight of and another single shot saw the man slumping into the dust. Brogan immediately leapt from his position in the roof on to a pile of loose straw and then he raced to stamp out the flames. He seized a besom standing against the wall and was beating the flames when he suddenly found Aaron alongside him, using his jacket as a beater. A few minutes later all the flames were out and Brogan and Aaron grinned at each other, panting for breath and mopping their sweaty foreheads.

Brogan listened; the shooting had stopped and

he looked out of the barn just in time to see six
riders heading away at great speed. He could
account for two, so he had to assume that the other
one had been shot by those inside the house.

'Looks like we beat 'em!' smiled Aaron.

'Looks like it,' agreed Brogan. 'Thanks for your
help; I don't reckon I could've doused the flames on
my own.'

'I seen what happened,' said Aaron. 'I thought
the others was copin' pretty well so I figgered I'd be
better used out here.' Sheriff Jarvis came out of the
house, closely followed by Jim Weston. They both
looked briefly at the bodies sprawled in the yard
before continuing to the barn. 'They is dead!'
assured Aaron. 'I already checked.'

'Good job you was here,' said Jim Weston. 'We'd
never've been able to put it out if it'd caught hold.'

'Looks like we only got three of 'em,' said Brogan.
'I saw six ride out an' there was nine rode in,
includin' Cartwright.'

'The one round the front looks pretty dead too,'
said Jarvis.

'Should've been all of 'em,' sighed Brogan. 'Pity
one of 'em ain't Cartwright, it might've saved a lot
of trouble, but I saw him ridin' out clearly enough.'

'Still, they've found out we mean business,' said
Jarvis, feeling quite proud of himself.

'Maybe that's a good thing an' maybe it ain't,'
said Brogan. 'One thing's certain, they'll be on
their guard from now on. Can't see you havin' no
more trouble from 'em today though, but it's
anybody's guess what they is gonna do next.'

'Probably go berserk an' try an' kill us all!'
muttered Jarvis.

'Most outlaws ain't that brave or stupid,' said Brogan. 'Sure they'll be lookin' for revenge, leastways Cartwright will; the others, if they is like most other outlaws, won't do nothin' that'll hurt them.'

'You seem to know a lot about such people,' observed Jarvis.

'I had me plenty of practice,' said Brogan. 'I've had to learn how folk think; it's kept me alive all this time.'

'Good job you was here,' said Weston. 'I don't reckon we'd've stood a chance if you hadn't been. Even if they hadn't killed us, this place would've been a pile of ash by now an' God knows what they would've done to May an' the girls.'

'Personally I think we gotta hit 'em while they is still reelin'!' said Aaron.

'They'll be expectin' just somethin' like that!' objected Jarvis.

'Aaron's got a point though,' said Brogan. 'We know they is now six men less but they is still strong enough to be confident that nobody ain't gonna take 'em on their own ground, so that's just where we'll take 'em!'

'I agree with that,' said Weston. 'Only trouble is gettin' up there: we'll never get within a mile of 'em without bein' seen.'

'I gotta give that some thought,' agreed Brogan. 'Right now we'd better be gettin' back to Apache Falls an' tell your wife that everythin's OK.'

'Mind if I use your other wagon to take these three back with me?' said Jarvis. 'It looks like their horses've bolted.'

'I'm comin' with you,' said Weston. 'C'mon, let's

load 'em up!'

Mayor Travers, whilst very pleased that no harm had come to any of them, appeared even more dismayed at the sight of the three bodies and shook his head sadly.

'I suppose you didn't have no option, but this is gonna make Cartwright even madder an' more unpredictable.' He stared hard at Brogan. 'What the hell brought you this way? Of all the places there must be to go, why pick on my town?'

'Somebody had to get lucky!' Brogan smiled.

'Smart arse!' grumbled Travers. 'Well, all I can say is since it was you what stirred up this hornets' nest, you can be the one what gets stung! I don't much like the idea of the sheriff workin' with you, but right now it looks like our options are very severely limited. Just remember though, whatever you decide to do, there's lots of innocent folk in this town that I don't want hurt on your account.'

'I can't guarantee nothin'!' said Brogan. 'If you is that worried maybe I'd better ride out now. I know I can get past 'em. If you want me to stay it's gonna cost somebody some food an' you'd better tell everybody to be ready to use their guns, just in case.'

'I'll see to some food,' offered Jarvis.

Travers grunted and nodded at Jarvis. 'An' I suppose I'd better put the word out about bein' prepared. OK, now I'm gonna leave you an' the sheriff to work out what you're gonna do. Whatever it is, I don't particularly want to know.'

'Typical of most mayors,' observed Brogan as Travers walked away. 'They is only too ready to take all the credit when things go right an' all the good things, but they just don't wanna know when the goin' gets hard.'

'Oh, don't take no heed of Travers,' said Jarvis, 'he ain't so bad. He's genuinely concerned about the town an' the folk what live hereabouts, which is more than could be said of the last mayor. OK, you heard the man, let's go talk tactics!'

'Only tactics I'm gonna talk at this moment in dynamite,' said Brogan. 'I got me an idea, but for the moment it don't concern anyone else. Can you get me, say, two dozen sticks?'

'Sure, shouldn't be no problem,' nodded Jarvis. 'What you got in mind?'

'Well I don't reckon that Cartwright is just gonna ride outa the safety of the pass, not just yet anyhow. He's lost six men an' I don't reckon he can afford to lose no more. He knows he's in a strong position an' like you say, a handful of men could hold that pass.'

'So what you got in mind?' Jarvis asked again.

'Obvious ain't it?' Brogan grinned. 'If they won't come to us, I guess we gotta go to them ...'

'That'd be plain suicide!' interrupted Jarvis.

'At least I go to them!' continued Brogan. 'Sure, it'd be askin' for trouble if we just rode in an' tried to shoot it out. I'm goin' up there by myself an' I'm gonna place the dynamite where it'll be most effective for when we'll need it – an' I reckon we is gonna need it!'

'How'd'ya mean, place it?'

'I got me a few ideas an' I'm always a believer in bein' prepared. Tryin' to place dynamite while you is under fire is plain stupid, if it's already there all you gotta do is light the fuse.'

'An' all you gotta do is get up there without bein'
seen, place it where you want it unseen an' then get
back here, again unseen!' sneered Jarvis. 'You able
to make yourself invisible or somethin'? It all
sounds too easy.'

'Yeh, that's all I gotta do!' replied Brogan, with a
broad grin. 'I ain't quite mastered the art of makin'
myself invisible, but I'm workin' on it. I've managed pretty well so far.'

Sheriff Jarvis looked very sceptical, but nevertheless, he had the feeling that this strange, dirty,
saddletramp knew exactly what he was doing.
'OK,' he said, eventually. 'I'll go fetch the dynamite. When you plannin' on goin' up there? It'll be
dark soon.'

'Yeh, it'll be dark soon,' agreed Brogan. 'Perfect
cover, they won't be able to see me ...'

'An' you won't be able to see them!'

'True, but then I'll know they is there somewhere,' replied Brogan, 'an' they won't know if I'm
around or not an' believe me, I can be quieter'n a
snake if I want to be. 'Sides, I been livin' out in the
open so long now I reckon I can hear a fly landin' on
a piece of shit a hundred yards away.'

'I believe you could too!' nodded Jarvis. 'OK, wait
here, I won't be long.'

'All sounds kinda risky to me,' said Aaron. 'You
want any help? I ain't so nimble as I used to be, but
I reckon I could still give most men a run for their
money.'

Brogan smiled and shook his head. 'No thanks,
Aaron, not this time. Next time I'll gladly count you
in, you an' anyone else who can handle a gun an' is
willin'.'

'Ain't too many of 'em gonna be that willin'!' muttered Aaron.

'I know that,' said Brogan, 'an' I ain't relyin' on 'em.'

Ten minutes later Jarvis returned with the dynamite, which Brogan stashed in his saddle-bags. He did not leave straightaway, waiting until it was almost dusk. Sheriff Jarvis did not question him further, knowing that Brogan himself was not too sure, but it was with a certain amount of trepidation that he watched the saddle-tramp slowly ride out of town and he could not help but wonder if he was doing the right thing. He sighed resignedly and knew that he was committed. From this point onward he had no options.

Clem Cartwright's mood was blacker than usual. He knew that he had been out-manoeuvred and out-thought and there was little doubt in his mind that the man responsible was the dirty saddle-tramp, although he had not actually seen him at the farm. The advice of his men was to ride into Apache Falls and burn the town to the ground and then clear out of the territory, but he was wise enough to realize that such a course of action was the recipe for disaster.

'So what you gonna do?' sneered one. 'You just gonna sit on your arse an' let 'em get away with it? You gotta teach 'em a lesson; you'll be the laughin' stock of the territory if you don't.'

'An' we is likely to end up dead if I listen to you!' responded Cartwright, bitterly. 'I know we gotta teach 'em a lesson but, more important, we gotta kill that saddlebum. With him outa the way the others won't know what to do.'

'One saddlebum shouldn't be no trouble!' said another.

'No, he shouldn't be!' grumbled Cartwright. 'But there's six dead men who might argue with you if they could. So far he's given us more trouble than all the folk in Apache Falls. He don't seem like no regular saddletramp; this one don't seem scared an' he seems to be able to handle a gun.'

'So you is gonna let one filthy saddlebum scare you off?'

'Nobody scares me off!' Cartwright reacted, angrily. 'But chargin' into Apache Falls ain't gonna achieve nothin', at this moment, maybe later. There's only one way outa Apache Falls, an' that's through here. He can't stay holed up there for ever, he's gotta make a move soon; types like him get restless after a couple of days.'

'He got back into town without us seein' him!' another outlaw pointed out. 'What's to say he can't get out again?'

'I already thought of that!' responded Cartwright. 'From now on we keep a twenty-four-hour watch, both through the pass an' the forest up top. He's gotta go through here or up there. You know the land up there; apart from the valley an' the forest, there ain't no other way. The cliffs on the other side are almost sheer an' at least a hundred feet. On his own he could probably get through, but unless he's ridin' a mountain goat, there ain't no way his horse can do it.'

'Twenty-four hours?' came the question. 'You mean we gotta watch all night?'

'I mean just that!' grated Cartwright.

SEVEN

Brogan reached the hills beyond the pass just as the moon broke from behind a bank of cloud, which gave him enough light to pick his way up the steep slopes. His one hope was that Cartwright had not thought about positioning a lookout this far away from the pass; if he had, the moonlight which now aided him would also aid anyone watching, and a man on horse would be easy to pick out. As he progressed up the slopes his confidence began to improve; so far he had neither sensed nor heard anything other than the normal sounds of the night, sounds he was well used to.

Eventually he reached the top and made his way toward the trees and he was quite certain that he had not been seen; he doubted very much if he would have been allowed to get this far if he had. The safety of the trees was reached and he followed the line of them, making sure that he kept in their shadow, until he reached the point where he judged he was opposite the lake.

'You gotta stay here, old girl,' he muttered to his horse and she seemed to be quite agreeable to the idea, immediately beginning to eat the lush grass.

Brogan tethered her with a long line, removed the
sticks of dynamite from his saddle-bags, putting
them into a small sack he had brought along, and
then spent some time studying the land ahead,
now well lit by the moonlight.

There were no trees between him and the lake,
although there was ample cover provided by the
numerous large rocks scattered about, behind any
one of which there could be an outlaw, but he
somehow did not think there would be, from
Cartwright's point of view it was not necessary.
He reasoned that if anyone was on lookout they
would be posted nearer the pass or the lake itself.
Nevertheless, he was very cautious in his
approach, listening for the slightest unusual
sound and keeping his keen eyes open for the
faintest of movements.

Twice he froze behind rocks; the first time when
he heard a scrape on some rock not too far away
and the second when a shadow ahead suddenly
moved. Both times the flurry proved to be caused
by deer, disturbed by his approach. He smiled to
himself, knowing that if there had been someone
else in the area, the deer would have sensed it
long before he had and would have been long
gone. As long as there were deer around he could
be reasonably certain that nobody else was.

The lake came into view quite suddenly, its
surface acting as a mirror for the moon, making it
stand out very clearly against an otherwise very
dark background. Brogan was still taking no
chances and he settled himself behind a large rock
and studied the area. He was in no great hurry; he
would wait until he was either absolutely certain

that there was no lookout or he had located him.
The obvious lookout points appeared to be
deserted, as did the shores of the lake, but still he
waited, his senses told him to, and in such
matters he always relied on his senses.

He had been watching and waiting for perhaps
half an hour when his senses proved him right; a
sudden flare of light from the old homestead by
the lakeside revealed the presence of someone just
inside the remains of the building. The light died
as quickly as it had flared up, but his keen eyes
detected the faintest glow as the lookout
apparently drew on a cheroot. Brogan decided to
remain where he was a little longer.

Taking the man out of action would have
presented no problem at all, but there was no way
of telling if, or when, he would be relieved or
checked on. Besides, at that precise moment it did
not suit Brogan's plans to either kill or disable the
man. If he did and it was discovered, they would
be certain to search the area and would probably
discover the dynamite. His plan was to secrete
several charges in the base of the dam, with the
intention of blowing the dam later, if it became
necessary.

The figure suddenly appeared from the ruins,
still drawing on a cheroot, and wandered slowly to
the water's edge and stooped down and appeared
to scoop some water into his mouth. After
standing up and gazing about, he slowly began to
walk around the edge of the lake, passing within
about twenty feet of Brogan, who resisted the
temptation to leap out and stab his knife into the
man's chest. The dark figure disappeared behind

a large rock, to reappear a minute later, his back
now towards Brogan.

The land on the far side of the lake sloped quite
steeply downwards away from the lake and,
unless the man kept to the water's edge, he would
be lost from view and, at the pace he was walking,
would be out of sight for perhaps five minutes. If
Brogan was to reach the dam he would have to get
past the ruins of the homestead. Once past it
there was no shortage of cover.

For a brief moment, Brogan thought that the
outlaw was going to keep to the edge of the lake,
but that meant wading through the mouth of the
stream which fed the lake, whereas if he went
further down he could jump across quite easily.
The man hesitated and then, much to Brogan's
relief, crossed further down and disappeared
down the slope. Brogan wasted no time; swiftly
and silently he made his way to the ruins, paused
briefly to check if the lookout had reappeared,
which he had not, and then raced for the shelter of
a group of large rocks directly above the dam.
About two minutes later the man reappeared on
the far side of the dam, walked about halfway
across and stood looking down for a few minutes.
What he was looking at, Brogan could not tell; as
far as he could see there was nothing down there
of particular interest, but the man was obviously
studying something.

Eventually the outlaw moved slowly across the
dam, looking up into the group of rocks where
Brogan was hidden, apparently looking straight
at him and for a moment Brogan was braced,
ready to act. However, the man turned along the

lakeside and slowly made his way back to the ruined homestead, where he propped his rifle against a wall, sat down and lit another cheroot. If Brogan had moved he would have been instantly seen, so all he could do was to crouch and wait and hope that the man would disappear inside the building.

After about ten minutes, Brogan became aware of a steady, rasping sound coming from the huddled outlaw and he allowed himself a wry grin – the lookout was asleep! He waited for about another five minutes to ensure that the man was well and truly asleep before making his move. Quickly and silently he slithered down the quite steep slope from his rocks to the base of the dam, crouched and listened and gave another grin as he heard the steady rasping of the outlaw's snores.

Brogan found himself having to work in total darkness, since the dam itself blocked out all moonlight, but that was no great problem and he was quickly able to locate suitable holes and loose rocks behind which to hide the dynamite. He spent about twenty minutes hiding twelve sticks of dynamite, ensuring that all the fuses were laid along cracks or grooves and all were laid the same way. With luck they would remain undetected and the odds were, that with a lookout having been posted at the dam and providing he could get away unseen, the outlaws would have no cause to suspect anything.

The snoring suddenly stopped; Brogan's senses screamed out; he flattened himself into the base of the dam and the ground and held his breath, at the same time firmly clasping his Colt in the event that he might need it. He knew that the man was standing on the dam above him and could not help but curse himself as he realized that the sack containing the dynamite was out in the open, though still in the shadow of the dam. To Brogan it was so obvious that he felt that anyone looking down would be certain to see it.

The figure coughed, noisily cleared his throat and spat an offensive glob of something down towards Brogan, but Brogan did not see or feel where it landed and at that precise moment it was the last of his worries. The man moved, kicked a loose rock which clattered down the side of the dam and coughed again. This time Brogan was painfully aware of exactly where the rock landed – right in the middle of his back! It took all his will-power not to at least grunt in pain.

Very slowly the figure moved on, in which direction Brogan could only guess at, but he thought it was back to the ruin. Whichever way it was, Brogan knew that he dare not move for quite some time, even the slightest sound from him was liable to attract the man's attention. After about ten minutes of listening he decided that it was probably safe enough to move, which he did very slowly, easing his cramped muscles. He smiled slightly as he heard the steady, rasping snore from somewhere above the dam.

Brogan thought about what he was going to do next and decided that achieving that objective was not going to be quite so simple as this one had been. His intention was to get to the narrow trail, on the far side of the outlaws' camp, which led up from the canyon, but to reach it he had to go almost through their camp. When he had observed them before, he had found that there was a sheer drop which prevented his going round, so all he had was a narrow piece of well-guarded rock.

He also had one more problem: he was now on the far side of the trail to their camp and, if his memory served him correctly, as it usually did, he would have to climb down sheer rock to the trail. Climbing down sheer rock in the daylight was difficult enough, but at night-time, especially when the moon was behind the rocks, the task seemed almost impossible to achieve without being heard. As he thought about it, he realized that the fact that the moon would be hidden was to his advantage, at least his progress down the sides would be that much harder for any observer to see.

The logical place to climb down was where the trickle of water seeping through and over the dam disappeared over the edge and he cautiously peered over. The easy route was down the narrow chimney formed by the erosion of the water, but after feeling down as far as he could, he decided that it was far too slippery. Slowly he made his way a little further along and eventually found another narrow chimney which, as far as he could tell, stretched the whole of the forty or so feet to the trail below.

'Oh well, Brogan,' he said to himself, 'if neither Cartwright nor the fall don't kill you, maybe you is in with a fightin' chance!'

'Hope you realize this is plain stupid,' he replied. 'We could've been well clear of here by now – broke but clear – this way we is liable to end up broke an' dead!'

'Then it won't matter none if we is broke,' he muttered; 'money ain't much use to a dead man, not so far as I know that is.'

'You is still bein' stupid!'

'Yeh, maybe I am,' he replied with a smile, 'but you can't say life is dull!'

'It'd sure make a change!'

Having had one of his regular conversations with himself, he slowly eased himself over the side, lowering himself until he was almost at full stretch finding a foothold. Very slowly and very gingerly, he began to climb down, making his way entirely by feel and not at all helped by the sack containing the other twelve sticks of dynamite stuffed into his shirt. He was about to discard the sack, let it drop to the trail, when he suddenly froze against the rock. The unmistakable sound of horses echoed in the still night, obviously heading his way. It seemed an eternity before two black shapes emerged round a bend in the trail. He was very thankful that he had not decided to drop the dynamite at the start of his descent or a few seconds earlier. The trail was very narrow at that point and, if nothing else, the horses may well have kicked the sack and drawn it to the riders' attention, if they had not seen it themselves.

'I reckon Clem's gone mad,' he heard one of them say, 'ain't nobody gonna do nothin' in the dark!'

'He reckons this saddletramp might just try an' get through,' came the reply.

'Personally I hope he's already gone,' came the

response. 'Sure would save us a whole lotta hassle.'

'You scared?'

'Scared? Hell no, it'd just make things a whole lot easier if Clem did let this saddlebum escape.'

'He's already taken out six of us, at least three of 'em by himself, maybe a couple of those at the farm as well for all we know.'

'Just what I mean; he's more trouble than he's worth. Maybe we'll get him, maybe we won't. One thing's for sure, it won't bother me none if he does get away an' it could save a few more men, maybe even you an' me. I hear he's mighty handy with a gun.'

'Maybe you is right!' came the agreement.

After what seemed like hours of hanging on to a narrow strip of rock – in reality only about two minutes – the men disappeared and Brogan was able to continue his descent, this time dropping the sack in the reasonable knowledge that other riders would not be along just yet.

'I gotta find the easier way back up!' he panted as he reached the bottom. There was an easier way, he had already used it, but exactly where it was he was not sure, but he would find it.

He looked about in the blackness and realized that he was boxed in, there was no way across the trail unless he was prepared for a long climb, so he decided to head towards where he knew their camp was. It was only a matter of about twenty-five yards but, had he encountered anyone who happened to ride through, there would have been no alternative but to shoot it out, and that would probably have been disastrous – for him!

Fortunately he met nobody and soon found his way across the trail, almost at the exact spot he had crossed before.

Finding his way to their camp was simple enough, a tell-tale red glow indicated their fire and very soon he was lying flat, overlooking them. He could see about ten men, some just huddled around the fire and others engaged in various activities. He resisted the great temptation to hurl the remaining dynamite among them, although in such a confined space it would certainly have caused a great deal of injury.

There was no way of telling exactly how many of them there were, since one would disappear and another would appear as they moved about. He eased himself from his prone position and slowly made his way to where he knew the horses were corralled, locating another man on the way.

Since they appeared to be covering all ways in and out of the pass, he reasoned that there must be at least one lookout keeping watch on the narrow trail which led up from the canyon and, before he dared do anything else, he had to locate him or them.

Keeping well to the cover of the rocks above the trail, and taking great care not to dislodge even the smallest loose stone, he slowly made his way past the horses and it was not until he was almost at the point where the trail widened out and started to descend towards the canyon that he located a lookout. As far as he could tell there was only the one and he was easy enough to see, highlighted by a shaft of moonlight and sitting with his back towards the camp and about twenty yards from where Brogan was.

Immediately before the trail widened out, it passed through a very narrow gully with sides about ten or twelve feet high and only about four feet wide, the perfect place to create a blockage. Brogan looked and felt about and smiled contentedly; even a single charge of dynamite was probably more than enough to bring down sufficient rock and earth, but a single stick might well be difficult to locate when the time came, so he secreted four of them, any one of which would do the job. Satisfied that he had achieved all he had set out to achieve, Brogan decided it was time to get back to Apache Falls.

Finding his way back to where he had left his horse presented no problem at all, the problem came as he neared the point where his horse was tethered. A sudden 'snort' made him stop and sink to the ground behind a rock.

Years of travelling with the same old horse meant that he could recognize the sound of her, even down to the way she walked and the sound of her hooves; in her way she was just as recognizable as any human. The 'snort' he had just heard was most definitely not made by his horse.

He knew exactly where she was tethered, although he could not see her, but he did hear her 'snort' and it sounded uneasy, which made him uneasy as well. Knowing that another horse was nearby but not having been able to place exactly where the sound came from, he crouched and watched and waited. For a full five minutes he waited and listened and once again a brief 'snort' was heard, but this time he was ready for it and was able to place the sound some twenty or so feet to the right of where his horse was tethered and that was near enough for him.

He was quite certain that he had not been seen, quite sure that had he been, there would have been some action by now. Having placed the horse was one thing, there was no guarantee that the rider would be anywhere near it, although the chances were that he was. The other thing was getting from where he was to the trees without being seen. Other than rocks there was no cover and a quick glance up at the sky showed that he was not going to get any help from cloud cover, there was not a single cloud to be seen. It seemed that he had two choices, remain where he was and wait for them to act or crawl on his belly using the rocks as cover.

Time was something Brogan had no shortage of, but he did not particularly want to stay where he was all night, so he decided to crawl. The process was very slow, taking the best part of twenty minutes before he could reach the trees behind where he suspected the man, or men, were hidden. Once among the trees things became considerably easier.

A brief survey soon located the horse, but there was no sign of its owner. It was at that moment that he became aware of another horse, this time seeming to be situated in almost the same spot as his own, which rather puzzled him and he started forward.

He was not sure whether to put it down to old age creeping up on him or pure carelessness,

whichever it was it made little difference to the
outcome. As a man who claimed to live by his wits
and to be able to hear the slightest noise, he must
have looked very foolish swinging upside down by
his ankle. He had fallen victim to one of the oldest
tricks in the book, the lasso tied to a branch or a
sapling, had trodden on the release mechanism
and before he knew what had happened he was
swinging helplessly.

There was a cry of triumph from somewhere
above his head and the words 'Gotcha, gotcha!'
which had a familiar ring to them.

'What the hell you playin' at Aaron?' croaked
Brogan. 'You could've got us both killed!'

'What am I playin' at?' demanded Aaron. 'You
shoulda come in the other way.'

'It's 'cos you was makin' so much noise I came
this way,' replied Brogan. 'Get me down outta this
contraption before the whole valley hears.'

'Didn't make a sound,' protested Aaron. 'How
d'ya know I was here?'

'Sure as hell didn't know it was you,' said
Brogan. 'Now get me down from here.'

'Hold your temper!' grumbled Aaron. 'Worked
though didn't it? Been a good many years since I
used that trick.' He pulled on the rope and
lowered Brogan to the ground, where Brogan
quickly freed himself. 'Maybe you ain't all you is
cracked up to be,' continued Aaron.

'Just what the hell are you doin' here?'
demanded Brogan, rubbing his ankle. 'I could've
killed you.'

'Not swingin' upside down like a monkey you
couldn't!' laughed Aaron.

'OK, OK!' grumbled Brogan, his pride more than slightly hurt at having been outwitted by an old soldier. 'That still don't answer the question of what you is doin' here.' He suddenly looked very alarmed. 'There ain't nobody else with you is there?' Aaron shook his head. 'Then who the hell does that other horse belong to?'

'Oh, him,' said Aaron, casually. 'He won't be no trouble, dealt with him hours ago.'

'Dealt with him?'

'Yeh, he's over here,' laughed Aaron, leading the way through a thicket to where the horses were tethered, and pointing. There was a very dead looking outlaw sprawled on the grass. 'Before you ask, he's dead,' continued Aaron. 'I ain't squeamish an' as far as I'm concerned the only good outlaw is a dead outlaw.'

'So what you doin' here?' asked Brogan, again.

'Figured you might just need some help,' replied Aaron, 'an' it seems I was right. I followed you about ten minutes after you'd gone. Mister, you sure ride slow, only way I could keep behind you was by stoppin'. Well, I found where you'd left your old horse easy enough an' decided to leave mine there too. Only trouble was I wasn't at all sure which way you'd gone. Anyhow, 'bout ten minutes after I'd arrived, I seen this feller here an' he saw the horses. I let him hide his horse an' then I killed him. Used a knife, I ain't stupid enough to use a gun up here.'

'Yeh, well thanks,' grunted Brogan. 'But I reckon I could've managed without your help.'

'Didn't expect no great thanks,' laughed Aaron, 'an' maybe you could've managed, providin' he'd've stayed an' waited for you to come back, but the chances are he'd've gone an' told the others an' then where would you've been?'

'Still alive I reckon,' said Brogan. 'I knew you was here didn't I? I'd've heard anyone else.'

'Yeh,' mused Aaron, 'gotta give you that. I know I didn't make a sound, so how'd'ya know?'

'I just knew!' Brogan grinned. He was not going to tell anyone how he knew these things. 'We'll have to take this feller back with us; if they find him it could spoil things.'

'Remember, he's mine,' said Aaron. 'I know there's a hundred dollars out on this one, dead or alive.'

'I reckon you earned it,' said Brogan. 'I only hope you live to spend it.'

'I earned it,' agreed Aaron. 'OK, Mister Saddlebum, what you been doin' out there?' He felt the sack which had been fastened around Brogan's shoulders. 'I'd say you used about half.'

'Go get this feller's horse an' I'll explain on the way back,' said Brogan.

'Still reckon I'm too old?' asked Aaron. 'That's what most folk think. Too old an' stupid they all say.'

'I don't recall sayin' you was too old,' said Brogan. 'Far as I'm concerned there ain't no such thing as too old for anythin'.'

'You got a plan then?' asked Aaron.

'Plan?' laughed Brogan. 'No, sir, never have no plans; only thing plans is good for is goin' wrong. I got me a few ideas though, an' I reckon they'll work …'

EIGHT

Sheriff Jarvis listened patiently to Brogan's ideas, but he did not seem over-impressed. 'An' you reckon four of us is enough to keep 'em penned in?' he said, shaking his head when Brogan had finished.

'Don't see why not,' replied Brogan. 'You said yourself a few men could hold out against an army up there ...' Jarvis nodded. 'Thing is, as I see it, while they could hold out a long time, the very thing what protects them is also their prison, they can't get out either, certainly not against a few, well-placed guns.'

'I guess that makes some kinda sense,' said Aaron, who had invited himself to the conversation. 'I reckon Jake'll be able to help out, I know he sure wants to, he's been practisin' with his left hand an' he ain't too bad at that.'

'Hand guns ain't gonna be much use,' said Brogan. 'As long as he can point a rifle an' squeeze the trigger, that's all that matters.'

'Rifle ain't no problem!' grinned Aaron.

'Seems a crazy idea to me,' sighed Jarvis, 'maybe that's why it just might work. OK, I'll go along with it. Jim Weston said to be sure an' call on him if we need him.'

'Then I reckon we'd better call on him,' said Brogan. 'The more guns we got the better. That makes four, five with me.'

'Could be there's a couple of others as'll join us,' said Jarvis. 'Wouldn't rely on too many of 'em though.'

'Like I said, the more guns the better. Even if they ain't good shots, Cartwright ain't gonna know that. Get as many as you can together. I'll leave all that to you; you know 'em, I don't. Right now though, I need me some shut-eye.'

'Jail's free,' offered the sheriff, with a broad grin.

'No thanks,' smiled Brogan. 'I'd feel safer outside. I'll be fine in the stable. My old horse is kinda used to my smell by now.'

'Yeh, maybe you're right at that!' sniffed Jarvis.

'What you sniffin' at?' asked Aaron. 'I can't smell nothin'.'

'That's only 'cos you smell worse'n Brogan here,' grinned Jarvis.

'Any of you seen Pete Smith?' Clem Cartwright asked his men. 'I ain't seen or heard hair or hide of him since last night.'

'Nobody's seen him,' came the reply. 'We figure he's decided to quit. Can't say as I blame him, it gets kinda borin' up here.'

'Borin' but safe,' Cartwright pointed out.

'Yeh, but we might as well be in prison since we can't go nowhere.'

'You can all ride out whenever you like,' said Cartwright, 'but I don't reckon Pete's done that. If that had been on his mind he'd've been after his share of what we got. Would any of you ride out just like that, empty handed?' They all shook their heads. 'Another thing,' continued Cartwright, 'his bedroll's still here. Looks like somethin's happened to him. I don't like it, he was supposed to be keepin' watch up in the valley.'

'You reckon this saddlebum's got through an' maybe taken out Pete?' asked one.

'If he has, then Pete's horse should still be wanderin' around up there. Two of you go an' take a look. If you see anythin' don't do nothin', just get back here fast. OK, those of you who didn't work last night get out there an' keep your eyes open. I dunno why, but I got me this feelin' that somethin's gonna happen. The rest of you might as well get some sleep while you can, but if anyone hollers or you hear shootin', you come runnin' double quick.' The men acknowledged the instructions and two of them volunteered to go and look for Pete Smith or his horse.

Cartwright's sense of unease increased; he could not explain why, but he was quite certain that something was going to happen and his unease was not helped by the fact that he knew there was absolutely nothing he could do to anticipate it, except wait.

'I reckon you're all crazy!' rasped Mayor Travers. 'What can seven of you possibly hope to do against them up there? I know somethin's gotta be done, but you stand no chance.'

'Then how about makin' it eight?' said Brogan. 'Join us; we can always use more guns.'

Travers looked rather uncomfortable. 'If there was any chance of success then I would,' he said, defensively, 'but I'm not in the business of committing suicide.'

'Then you come up with some better idea,' Brogan said again. 'As far as I'm concerned, Mr Mayor, it's a case of put up or shut up, 'Course, if it'd suit you better I'll just ride out an' leave you to it.'

'I didn't say we don't want your help,' blustered Travers, 'but this idea of yours seems pure madness.'

'You is dead right about that!' laughed Brogan. 'I must be bloody crazy, it's most likely me what'll end up gettin' killed!'

'That's the way you want to play it,' Sheriff Jarvis pointed out.

'You is wrong about that!' sneered Brogan. 'It ain't the way I want it, but it looks like that's the way it's gotta be.'

'OK! OK!' conceded Mayor Travers. 'Have it your way. Personally I reckon I'd better tell Collins he's gonna be in business.'

'Collins?' queried Brogan.

'Ted Collins, undertaker!'

'That's what I like to see,' said Brogan, 'a mayor what's full of confidence. OK, it seems we gotta be thankful for the two more volunteers we got.' He looked at the two youths, both aged about eighteen years. 'You two quite certain you wanna go through with this?'

'Anythin's better'n sittin' on our arses an' lettin' 'em walk all over us,' nodded Tony Robbins, whose father owned the corn and seed store.

'Same goes for me,' agreed the other youth, Ben Pearson, the veterinarian's son. 'We been sayin' all along that somebody oughta do somethin'; in fact we volunteered for a posse, but the sheriff couldn't raise nobody else.'

'Pity you had to shoot up my gun hand,' said the old man, Jake. 'Still, I asked for it I reckon. I been practisin' though an' I reckon I'm good enough with my left hand.'

'You'll be usin' rifles,' said Brogan. 'Reckon you can manage one?'

'Nothin' to it!' grinned Jake, suddenly raising his rifle to his shoulder. 'My finger still works!'

'Neither of us own a rifle,' Ben Pearson pointed out. 'My pa knows what I'm doin' but he won't lend me his, not that it's much use, too old.'

'My pa was the same,' said Tony Robbins.

'No problem,' said Jarvis. 'You can have one from the rack over there. I reckon I gotta supply the bullets for everyone as well.'

Tony Robbins grinned sheepishly. 'Shouldn't we be sworn in as deputies or somethin'?' He puffed out his chest. 'I kinda fancy myself with a deputy's star.'

'It would make it all legal,' said the mayor; 'just the same as if you were a posse, which I suppose you are.'

'OK,' smiled Jarvis. 'I got me some deputies' stars here somewhere.' He fumbled in a drawer and found a handful of badges, which he tossed on to the table. The two youths eagerly grabbed one each and pinned them proudly to their shirts. That left one each for Aaron and Jake and one over. Brogan decided that he did not want to wear it.

'Weston can have it,' he said.

'We gotta collect him on the way,' said Jarvis, picking up the badge.

'YOU gotta collect him,' said Brogan. 'You all know what you gotta do so I'll leave you to it. Don't worry 'bout me; I'll be in position before you, so just keep 'em occupied as soon as you get there.'

Brogan left the office and Mayor Travers went through the formalities of swearing the others in as deputies.

Brogan followed the river southwards, leaving it just before it passed the Weston farm and then he circled round until he found his way up into the hills, eventually coming out into the high valley about half a mile further down than he had before. This time he chose to ride among the trees until he came to the same small clearing where he had left his horse before and tethered her again.

From this point onward, the routine would be much the same as before, except that he had to reach the camp first and, if the others were doing their job properly, the outlaws would be far too busy to notice him. After checking for signs of life, he made his way towards the lake, following almost exactly the same line as before, but he had only travelled about fifty yards when a sudden flight of birds and a lone deer bolting out of the forest behind him made him dive for cover.

Two riders suddenly appeared, heading more or less straight for him. 'I could've sworn I heard a horse!' one of them called.

'Ain't no sign of life out here,' came the reply. 'I reckon it must've been that deer you heard. Pete's been long gone. I don't care what Clem says, I know he was fed up with this set-up.'

'I still reckon it was a horse!' insisted the first man. 'You is right though, there ain't no horse out here. Come on, we'll try over there.' He pointed in the general direction where Brogan had left his horse.

'We is wastin' our time!' grumbled the other. 'He's run out I tell you. Can't say as I blame him either, I'm thinkin' about it too.'

'That's up to you, come on, give it another half-hour then we'll pack it in an' get back.'

'Half an hour, no more!' came the grumbling agreement.

Brogan remained where he was as the two riders veered away and headed back towards the trees. It was quite obvious that they would discover his horse and equally obvious that they would realize that it did not belong to this 'Pete' he had heard them mention. He did not have long to wait before they did discover his horse.

The two men suddenly burst out of the tree cover and once again headed in his direction. 'He can't be far away!' he heard one call.

'Not far enough!' muttered Brogan, realizing that he had no option but to kill them. He would have to chance the shots being heard. Two shots rang out, echoing off the rocks and the two riders fell from their horses like rag dolls. The shots also disturbed large numbers of birds, which would have given his position away to any observer, but there was nothing he could do about that except keep his eyes and ears on the alert.

He did not break cover straight away, just in

case the commotion had attracted the attention of someone, but after about five minutes he was reasonably satisfied that nobody was coming to investigate. He checked the bodies and grunted with satisfaction at the sight of a neat hole in each temple. The bodies he left where they were, but the horses, which had stopped a short distance away, he led back amongst the trees and tethered alongside his own. He then resumed his journey.

He had almost reached the lake when he heard the echo of gunfire from the direction of the pass. This time, the expected lookout in the old ruin rushed to the edge of the pass and called out. Brogan could not hear what was said, but the figure suddenly disappeared down into the pass. At least it saved Brogan the problem of disposing of him.

Jake and Aaron, as instructed, made no attempt to conceal themselves as they followed the trail up from the canyon towards the outlaws' camp and this very fact caused some consternation amongst those watching.

'I know them two,' said one of the three lookouts. 'They is those stupid ex-cavalry soldiers. What they doin' comin' this way?'

'Hanged if I know,' replied one of the others. 'Maybe they've decided to quit Apache Falls.'

'Could be, but why the hell should they come this way?'

'Because they is stupid?' came the suggestion.

'What the hell they doin' now?' exclaimed the third lookout. Jake and Aaron had suddenly turned off the trail and disappeared behind some large rocks.

'Better call Clem!' instructed the first lookout. 'Somethin' ain't right.'

'They ain't right in the head, that's for sure,' grinned one of the others, climbing down and returning to the camp.

'I had me this feelin' that somethin' was goin' to happen,' said Clem Cartwright as he joined the lookouts, 'but this ain't nothin' like I expected. Where are they now?'

'Still behind them rocks,' came the reply. 'Don't know what they is playin' at, but it don't seem right to me.'

'Ain't no way of tellin' what them two crazy guys is up to,' said Cartwright. 'Only one way to find out I suppose ...' He turned to three of his men who had come to see what was happening. 'You three get out there an' flush 'em out an' bring 'em here.'

'Supposin' they don't wanna come?' asked one.

'You don't give 'em no choice,' grunted Cartwright. 'If they start shootin', you just make sure you get 'em, preferably alive, but kill 'em if you have to.'

'No problem!' grinned one of the men. 'Come on, let's go get 'em, they shouldn't be no problem.'

The three men had gone about a hundred yards when a shot rang out and one of them fell to the ground, clutching his shoulder.

Sheriff Jarvis, Tony Robbins and Ben Pearson met up with Jim Weston and the four of them rode to the pass, again making no attempt to hide their approach.

'That's as far as you go!' a voice echoed above them.

'It's as far as you go!' replied Jim Weston. His single shot was true and if the shot did not kill the lookout, the forty-foot fall almost certainly did. The four men leapt off their horses and dived for cover as a hail of bullets raised dust around them.

'What the hell they think they is doin'?' another lookout called to his remaining companion.

'Dunno!' came the reply. 'One thing's for sure though, they sure mean business!'

'You keep 'em pinned down! I'm gonna tell Clem!'

There was no need for him to tell Cartwright, the shooting had been heard at the camp and for a moment Cartwright was at a loss as to what to do.

'Well don't you all just look at me!' exploded Cartwright. 'Get your butts down there an' find out!'

In the meantime, the three men sent to deal with Jake and Aaron had managed to make their way back. 'Looks like they all gone mad!' panted one. 'I reckon they is tryin' to drive us out!'

'This is all that saddlebum's doin'!' snarled Cartwright. 'You five keep them two idiots occupied, I'm goin' to see what's happenin'!' He mounted his horse and raced to the head of the pass. 'How many of 'em?' he called out.

'Four, maybe five,' replied the lookout.

Cartwright shook his head. 'Don't see what only a handful of 'em can hope to achieve. Is that saddlebum one of 'em?'

'Don't know for sure, but I don't reckon he is!'

Cartwright looked nervously around. 'I got me

this feelin' that he ain't one of 'em, an' I got me this feelin' that he's around somewhere.'

Brogan was around; in fact he was, at that moment, overlooking the camp, having used the commotion to climb down into the pass and cross the trail and river to secrete himself above them.

Cartwright rode back to the camp just as the first explosion thundered and reverberated around the high rocks. Three other explosions followed in fairly quick succession, the falling rocks very quickly blocking the trail between the camp and where Jake and Aaron were hidden, which had been the intention, denying the outlaws one escape route. After a brief moment to dismount from his horse and grab something from his makeshift tent, Cartwright suddenly rode quickly out of the camp and headed for the other end of the pass. This went unnoticed by Brogan, who had rapidly made his way back across the trail and was climbing back to the lake.

He had expected his climb to be easy, assuming that everyone was fully occupied down below, but as his head looked over the top, a shot, immediately followed by dull thud close to his head made him curse and duck down. If anyone below had seen him he would have been a sitting target, but he was in luck, even though various figures were milling around, he went unnoticed.

Gingerly he peered over the edge again, just in time to see a shadowy figure disappearing into the huddle of rocks immediately above the dam. There was no way of telling if the figure stayed there or moved on, and Brogan was not prepared to chance it. Instead he climbed back to the trail and made his way further along until he was sure he was behind the point where the man was hidden, and then climbed again. This time he did make it to the top without incident.

The rocks were some twenty yards away, but there was no sign of the figure he had seen, although the chances were that he was there. Very slowly he edged his way forward, ever ready for that slight movement which would give away the position of the man, but it did not come and he soon made the safety of the rocks. After a short time listening and watching, he detected the slightest movement to his left.

The man had no chance; Brogan's knife flashed in the air briefly before slicing into the man's throat. 'Messy!' grumbled Brogan. 'Maybe you shoulda stayed down there with the others.' He checked his surroundings again and was satisfied that there was nobody else before he made his way to the dam.

It was not so much the sound of the explosions that persuaded the outlaws confronting Sheriff Jarvis and the others to abandon the idea, but the low, menacing rumble that followed the explosions. The rumble grew rapidly louder and suddenly the highest placed lookout yelled down to the others, at the same time attempting to jump from his pinnacle for more secure ground. In the event he only succeeded in slipping and crashing down to the trail.

'Get the hell outa here!' yelled Jarvis. 'He's blown the dam!'

There was no fear of being shot by the outlaws, who were far too concerned with their own fate, and they managed to scramble, with their horses, for higher ground.

Inside the pass, men were frantically trying to climb to safety before the wall of water crashed down on them. A few did manage to reach high rocks, but the majority were dragged under as the water hit them, sweeping them mercilessly and painfully along the trail and through the narrow entrance, where the water immediately spread over the flat ground, depositing bodies.

The four men from Apache Falls could only watch and wait, wait for the torrent of water to subside and, when it did, Jarvis instructed them to pick up any survivors. Of the fourteen bodies they found, four were already dead, four were close to death, having been battered against the rocks on their enforced journey, and six, although gasping for breath, seemed little the worse for their experience. Very quickly, all were rounded up, almost grateful to their captors.

Brogan watched with grim satisfaction as the flow of water slowly eased to a steady trickle and then he descended into the pass. At the camp he found two more dead bodies, trapped as the tide of water filled the hollow and found that three others had given themselves up to Jake and Aaron, who were even then busily tying them up.

'Told you it'd work!' he called to the two old men. 'Get them three back to town, we can collect the others later.'

He searched the camp for the box he knew to contain the money they had taken from the citizens of Apache Falls, and cursed slightly when he could not find it. Of all the horses penned nearby, four were dead and the others, their eyes bulging with terror, were pulling frantically at their tethers. He decided to leave them where they were, knowing that with the danger past, they would soon calm down.

He made his way slowly along the pass, sensing that there would be one or two survivors and quickly located three, huddled together on a ledge some thirty feet up. They did not appear to be armed, or to want to offer any resistance, but his rifle was ready, just in case.

'You up there, come on down!' he called. 'You is beaten; ain't no sense in gettin' yourselves killed now!'

'Bastard!' spat one of them. 'Clem said it was you what was behind all this.'

'Yeh, right on both counts I reckon,' laughed Brogan. 'You comin' down or do I have to shoot you where you are?'

'Since we ain't got no guns an' nowheres to hide, I guess we got no choice!' came the echoing reply. Slowly and painfully, the three men climbed down and were herded towards the entrance, where they were met by Jarvis and the others.

'We can account for fourteen here,' Jarvis informed Brogan. 'How many more are there?'

'Your fourteen an' these three, three what have given up to Jake and Aaron, two dead up at the camp an' three more I can account for, that makes twenty-five.'

'Twenty-five!' said Jarvis, rather surprised. 'I didn't reckon there was that many.'

'That makes almost thirty of 'em in total,' said Tony Robbins, 'takin' into account the ones what was killed before.'

'I can count!' muttered Jarvis. 'Cartwright ain't here, you found him up there?'

'Nope!' replied Brogan. 'I reckon he's done a bunk, taken all their money too.'

'Our money!' corrected Jim Weston.

'Yeh, your money an' mine!' grinned Brogan. 'Still, I reckon most of these got prices on their heads, maybe even enough to compensate everyone.'

'I know some of 'em have,' agreed Jarvis. 'I reckon it'd be only right if we was to offer the reward money to you; if it hadn't been for you we'd never've done this.'

'Mighty generous of you,' smiled Brogan, 'but I don't want all of it. All I want is what they took an' maybe a couple of hundred besides.'

Jarvis smiled and shook his head. 'You know, I kinda figured you'd say somethin' like that. I guess you ain't a feller who needs too much money.'

'Just enough to get me by,' nodded Brogan. 'Okay, let's get this lot back to town. You can organize a party to come out an' collect the dead an' those horses what is still alive. Right now I gotta get back up there an' collect my old horse.'

'Meet you in town,' said Jarvis. 'Okay, you lot!' he addressed the bedraggled outlaws, 'start walkin'!'

NINE

The atmosphere in Apache Falls was almost a carnival one, the saloon was suddenly bulging with customers and the local women were all gathered in the tea-room of the only hotel. As ever, however, there was one face which did not seem to find any cause for celebration, that of Mayor Travers.

The small jail of Apache Falls, although comprising two cells, had not been designed with any thought in mind other than to accommodate a few drunks on a Saturday night. Now, both cells were crammed full and Mayor Travers shook his head sadly. It was not so much the overcrowding which either saddened or worried him, it was the absence of one face amongst them all.

'You didn't get Cartwright!' he complained. 'You should've got Cartwright, he was the main one. There ain't no knowin' what he's liable to do now. Seems he got clean away with all our money too.'

'An' just how much of that money was yours?' sighed Brogan, barely able to control his rising impatience with the mayor.

'Well ... I ...' faltered Travers, 'I gotta admit I didn't lose no money to 'em, but there was a good many what did.'

'An' they all seem quite happy that we got rid of the threat,' Brogan pointed out. 'Seems the only one who's complainin' is the one what didn't lose nothin'! Mister Mayor, for the past few months you been complainin' you couldn't get through the pass, now you got a clear run through an' all the outlaws is either dead or in jail, 'ceptin' one, and all you can do is complain that he got away! Maybe I shoulda left you to sort 'em out by yourselves. Anyhow, I reckon there's a fair bit of reward money to come; I can't see any of this lot not havin' prices on their heads. Maybe you'll even recover what you all lost an' a bit more.'

'Maybe we will,' grumbled Travers. 'We ain't had time to work out how much it all comes to yet, an' there's sure to be a good many what we don't know about, which means we'll have to check an' we can't do that yet, the telegraph line is still down.'

'I reckon that can be repaired,' Brogan sighed. 'Anyhow, whatever it all comes to, you gotta take off two hundred an' eighty dollars.'

'Two hundred an' eighty?' queried Travers.

'Yeh, two hundred an' eighty,' Brogan confirmed, with a faint smile on his lips. 'Sheriff an' me agreed I'd take two hundred for my part from the reward an' the other eighty is what I lost.'

'I agree to the two hundred,' sighed Travers, 'but what you lost to Cartwright you gotta stand yourself.'

'Two hundred an' eighty!' sneered Brogan. 'If'n you wanna be awkward about it, I can easily claim my rightful share of the reward, which'll come to a darn sight more!'

'If you want to be strictly legal,' Travers laughed, a little unsure of himself, 'sheriffs an' deputies ain't allowed no part of any reward on account they was only doin' their duty.'

Brogan laughed loudly. 'Then I guess that means I'm entitled to all of it! Think about it, Mister Mayor I was the only one what wasn't sworn in as a deputy!'

Mayor Travers looked in horror at the dishevelled saddletramp standing sneeringly in front of him and eventually shrugged his shoulders. 'I guess you got me over a barrel. Okay, two hundred an' eighty.'

'Thought you'd see sense,' grinned Brogan.

A few hours later, the last of the bodies had been brought into town and the telegraph wire had been repaired, under the supervision of the officious little telegraph clerk, who was quite certain that nobody was capable of repairing the wire without him.

Later, surrounded by anxious faces, the clerk proceeded to make great show of tapping out the first message to leave Apache Falls for many weeks. There was an equally anxious wait for the answering message to come through and there was a great sigh of relief when the machine chattered into life. From that point onwards there was more or less continuous traffic along the wire, mostly with details of outlaws the sheriff could not identify. Brogan's assumption that all of the outlaws would have prices on their heads proved correct and the final tally for those they had came to almost $12,000 and had they been able to add Cartwright to the list, it would have been boosted by another $3,000.

Almost grudgingly, Mayor Travers handed Brogan his $280 and, under the expectant gaze of most of the townsfolk, was more or less forced to make a speech, thanking Brogan for the part he had played.

'Guess you'll be movin' on now,' said Sheriff Jarvis, when the crowd had dispersed and Travers had hastily disappeared.

'Reckon so,' agreed Brogan. 'I'll be off at first light in the mornin'. I already stayed a lot longer'n I intended, 'sides, there don't seem much to do round here.'

'You're right about that!' Jarvis smiled, almost happily. 'That's the way we like it. I reckon we've had enough excitement to last a lifetime; folk round here ain't used to it.'

'I certainly won't be sorry to be on my way,' said Brogan. 'Thanks for the money, although if it'd been left to Travers I wouldn't've got any.'

'Travers ain't so bad!' laughed Jarvis. 'Got the welfare of this town at heart, that's the main thing.'

'That right about what he said, you an' the others not bein' able to collect the reward money?'

'Strictly speakin', yeh!' grinned Jarvis. 'But there ain't nothin' stoppin' him payin' us all a bonus! Only thing is, I'm kinda surprised you didn't ask for more, you was entitled.'

'I told you before,' Brogan grinned. 'I ain't got that much use for a lot of cash. I ain't greedy!'

Brogan rode quietly out of Apache Falls just as dawn was breaking and only just before the first citizens were up and about. He preferred things that way, no fuss – not that there was normally any fuss at his departure, more often than not only relief.

The pass still had the evidence of what had happened, but he decided to check where the camp had been for the final time, just in case the box was still there. He disturbed about twenty buzzards greedily gorging themselves on the now stinking corpses of the dead horses. He grimaced slightly but left the birds to their disgusting meal; it would not be long before all that remained of the horses would be the bleached bones.

Having satisfied himself that the box was not there, he continued his journey through the pass, after which he headed north-west, for no other reason than that was the way he fancied going. In the morning he was just as likely to change his mind and head south or even east. With nowhere to go, it often as not made little difference which way he went, even round in circles if it took his fancy.

He travelled all that day without seeing a sign of life except the odd bird, a few lizards and the ever-present flies, which seemed to come out of nowhere. Not that he covered any great distance, neither time nor distance held any great meaning for him. That night he camped alongside a small river and was more than a little surprised to find evidence of another traveller having passed that way fairly recently. His immediate thought was that it had been Clem Cartwright, but other than that, he did not give it much further thought.

The following morning, he leisurely continued

his journey, a journey that had no real purpose or objective, and that was the way he liked it, free to please himself. At about noon he came upon a staging-post used by the stage-coach company and decided that a cooked meal and a glass of beer would be more than welcome.

'Second ... er ... traveller in two days,' commented the owner, not at all sure what to call Brogan. 'Don't usually get two in a month, 'ceptin' the stages.'

'Place must be gettin' popular,' said Brogan. 'Don't tell me, this other feller, was he a little guy but with a chest like a barrel, moustache ...'

'No, big guy he was,' interrupted the man. ''Bout as tall as you, 'bout the same build as well, no moustache either.'

'Ain't no feller I know,' said Brogan. The description he had given did not fit Clem Cartwright at all, but the description the owner of the post had given certainly did.

'You lookin' for this guy?' The question was not unexpected.

'Not particularly,' replied Brogan, which was true, 'an' certainly not the feller you saw. Where does this trail go?'

'There's two trails!' corrected the man. 'This is a mighty important post ...' – He puffed out his chest, proudly – 'right on a crossroad used by two stage-coach companies – I work for both of 'em. North-east leads to Denver, north-west to Salt Lake City, south-west, Phoenix, an' south-east, Albuquerque ... where you headed?'

'Don't rightly know,' admitted Brogan. 'I never know till I gets there, only thing is, I ain't never got there yet.'

'Guessed you was a drifter. Funny that, the feller what was through here yesterday was goin' on about some drifter, sayin' as how he'd like to kill him ... You ain't that drifter are you?'

'I may look like a madman, but do you really reckon I is one?' laughed Brogan. 'I would have to be outa my mind if I was followin' someone who wanted to kill me, wouldn't I?'

'Reckon so,' agreed the man. 'I didn't ask too many questions; I long since found out it don't pay an' this guy sure didn't look the type to be messed with. I know my wife was kinda glad when he rode out. Didn't even want to take her ...' – He looked hard at Brogan – 'it's one of the services we got. Maud don't mind an' the extra money is sure useful. You fancy a woman, after you've eaten that is?'

Having seen the size of Maud, Brogan was even less inclined to take up the offer, but he idly enquired the price and was told 'Two dollars,' which seemed quite reasonable, but another glance at Maud indicated that it was probably a fair price, so he declined.

'Which way this other feller go?'

'North-east, to Denver.'

'Then I reckon I'll head north-west,' Brogan grinned. 'If this guy's got a thing about saddletramps, I don't fancy meetin' up with him.'

'Makes sense, I suppose,' nodded the man. 'Now, what you gonna eat? We got stew an' we got beef steak.'

'I kinda fancy a steak,' replied Brogan. 'You got some beer?'

'We got beer an' whisky. I keep a little gin but that's mainly for the women on the stage-coaches, seems most of 'em can't take whisky.'

'Havin' tasted most the stuff what passes for whisky out here, I can't say as I blame 'em,' smiled Brogan. 'I know it sure takes the linin' off my stomach, so what the hell it does to a woman's I hate to think.'

'I got me some of the real stuff,' said the man, proudly. 'Best Scotch, all the way from Scotland.'

'No thanks, I'll stick to beer,' said Brogan. 'I ain't much of a whisky man anyhow.'

'Suit yourself,' replied the man, looking hard at Brogan again. 'I don't mean no offence, mister, but since you admit to bein' a saddletramp an' 'cos I long since learned from experience that most saddletramps only want somethin' for nothin', you got some cash on you?'

'Yeh, some saddletramps give the rest of us a bad name,' Brogan laughed. 'Sure, I got more'n enough. How much?'

'Dollar an' a quarter,' said the man, a little nervously.

Brogan dug into his pocket and pulled out a handful of change and counted out the necessary money and handed it to the man. 'Satisfied?' he asked.

'Sure thing!' gulped the man, almost snatching the money. 'Price includes feed for your horse too, I'll see to it.'

Instructions were called to Maud and he disappeared outside to tend to Brogan's horse. Maud waddled into the dingy room and tried to look seductively at Brogan.

'How do you like your steak?' she asked.

'Rare,' replied Brogan.

'Rare it is,' she smiled. 'That how you like your women too?'

'Yeh, very rare,' replied Brogan. 'As rarely as possible.'

'Suit yourself!' she huffed. 'I can't say as I really fancy a stinkin' saddletramp either!' With that she stomped off back to the kitchen and angrily clattered some pots and pans.

Eventually his meal was thrust in front of him and, much to his surprise, he found that it actually tasted quite good, although the vegetables defied identification. The nearest he could say was swede, heavily peppered, but still quite tasty. After finishing the meal, he was again asked if he wanted to sample the delights that Maud had to offer, but again he declined and collected his horse to take the trail to the north-west.

There seemed little doubt in his mind that the man who had passed by the day before had been Clem Cartwright but, since he had recovered his money, he had no intention of chancing his luck in going after him. Despite the fact that he found himself involved in trouble with regular monotony, he never, or very rarely, actively looked for it.

Towards dusk he came upon a fork in the trail; it was quite obvious which was the main trail to Salt Lake City, but this side trail was also fairly well worn, indicating that there must be some sort of settlement ahead, but just how far ahead was another question but one that did not matter to him.

Since he had no particular desire to go to Salt

Lake City, he decided that he may as well follow the new trail, especially since one place was as good as another to him. After a very short time he found himself entering very familiar territory.

It was not the actual territory itself which was familiar – as far as he knew he had never been along this trail before – but he felt very much at home in the bleak, twisted, sandswept land that lay ahead. Just before nightfall he found a water-hole and a signpost which indicated that the town of Big Rock lay ten miles ahead – he decided that the water-hole was preferable to Big Rock.

The following morning he set off again, with little choice of direction other than back the way he had come – which seemed a waste of time and effort. It had been his intention to avoid Big Rock but, to his slight dismay, he found that it proved impossible. He had travelled along a narrow valley, which obviously became a river at certain times of the year but was now completely dry, with sheer sides rising to about eighty feet and the nearer he got to Big Rock, the more he found it impossible to scale the sides.

Big Rock obviously took its name from the huge, pointed rock which rose some sixty feet above the valley sides. The town itself straddled the entrance of the valley and, as far as Brogan could see, there was no alternative but to go through.

Quite why he was not sure, but as he rode into the town his senses screamed out to him that something was wrong. Perhaps it was the way the main street suddenly cleared of people, he could not really tell, but something was not right.

'Let's get through here fast!' he muttered to his

horse, to which she nodded in agreement.

His intention may have been to ride through, but fate decreed otherwise; suddenly he heard the thunder of hooves and looked round to see riders closing in on him from both sides of the street. He realized that his old horse was no match for any of them and he also realized that to attempt to go for his gun would only result in his certain death and he was not ready to die yet, especially when he did not know the reason.

'Hold it right there!' commanded a burly looking man with a star on his vest which indicated the sheriff. 'Thought you'd try an' fool us did ya?'

Brogan did not raise his hands, but simply sat and waited as they surrounded him. 'If I knew what or who I was tryin' to fool I might be able to answer that question,' he said as they stared at him.

'Don't come the funnies with me!' snapped the sheriff, getting off his horse. 'You know darned well what I mean. Keep him covered,' he ordered his men. 'If he so much as moves an eyelid, kill him!'

'You ain't got no need to shoot,' said Brogan. 'I ain't about to try nothin', I ain't that stupid!'

'Stupid enough to get caught!' sneered the sheriff, holding his rifle steadily at Brogan's chest. 'Drop your guns, real slow an' any knives you got.'

'I ain't arguin',' sighed Brogan, gingerly pulling his Colt from its holster and dropping it on to the ground, following it with his knife and then his Winchester. 'Now, maybe you'll tell me what this is all about. A man's got a right to know.'

'You got no rights in this town!' barked the

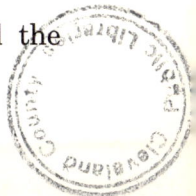

sheriff. 'Off your horse!' Brogan obeyed, realizing that at that precise moment he was not going to get a sensible answer. 'Okay, now walk!' commanded the sheriff again. 'Jail's thataway ...' – he indicated the street behind him – 'an' remember, you try an' run an' you won't get five yards.'

'I gave up runnin' a long time ago,' replied Brogan, walking down the street in front of the sheriff.

The street which had so miraculously become deserted when he had entered Big Rock was now, just as miraculously, filled with surly-looking people, some of whom were already demanding that he be 'Strung up!' A deputy went ahead and opened the sheriff's office and then the single cell inside, into which Brogan was unceremoniously pushed.

'Okay!' said Brogan. 'You got me safely locked up, now would you mind explainin' what's goin' on?'

'Don't come the innocent with me!' snapped the sheriff. 'You know only too well. Nice trick though, you sure got a nerve, comin' back this way.'

'Sheriff!' sighed Brogan, 'I don't even pretend to understand what all this is about. As for me comin' back this way, as you put it, I ain't never been nowhere else to come back from.'

'So you say!' snarled the sheriff. 'All I can say mister if it ain't you then you got a double. Widder Carter's description fits you perfectly.'

'Widder Carter?' asked Brogan. 'Might've known there'd be a woman behind this some-where. Trouble is with descriptions they can fit almost anybody. Some of the men with you look pretty much the same as me.'

'You can try an' wriggle out of it if you like!' laughed the sheriff, 'but all the men in this town is known to her, so she wouldn't make a mistake like that!'

'Okay, so what am I supposed to have done to this Widder Carter?'

'Saddlebum is how she described the man an' she gave a pretty good description, even though you damned nigh killed her. At the moment you is held on a charge of rape an' assault an' if she don't pull through you'll swing for murder.'

'I hear the penalty for rape is also hangin',' said Brogan, 'so it ain't gonna make much difference.'

'No, it ain't gonna make no difference!' laughed the sheriff.

'Don't suppose you is gonna believe me if I say I ain't never met or heard of this Widder Carter,' sighed Brogan.

'No, it ain't gonna make no difference!' sneered the sheriff.

'Then all I can hope is that she don't die,' said Brogan. 'At least she'll be able to identify me, at least she'll be able to say it wasn't me.'

'That's your only hope!' laughed the sheriff. 'Maybe now she'll learn that she shouldn't be livin' out there on her own.'

'How bad is she?' Brogan prompted.

'Bad enough, for all you should care!' said the sheriff. 'Last I heard the doc reckons it's touch an' go.'

'Then let's hope it's "go"', muttered Brogan, sincerely.

TEN

Brogan realized that nothing he could say or do was going to influence Sheriff Michael Gordon – as he had discovered the sheriff was named – in any way at all. As far as this particular enforcer of the law in and around Big Rock was concerned, a crime had been committed and the culprit apprehended and locked safely in his jail. The fact that Gordon, during his six years as sheriff, had never had to deal with anything more serious than two farmhands trying to shoot each other on one occasion – and both had been too much under the influence of drink to be of any danger to each other and had to be locked up more to protect other people – did not convince him, or raise any doubts, that possibly his prisoner was telling the truth. This was a big day for him and he intended to make the most of it.

The townsfolk of Big Rock too seemed satisfied that the rapist had been caught and, since they were well away from the influence of what other organized law there was, were only too eager to see what they considered quick and proper justice, in the form of a hanging. However, to his credit – at least as far as Brogan was concerned – Sheriff

Michael Gordon insisted on a trial.

'We gotta do things proper!' he told everyone.
'The law says every man's got a right to a fair an'
proper trial afore he's hung.' The assumption that
hanging was inevitable rather detracted from the
fairness of any trial in Brogan's eyes. The trial
was set for the following morning – swift justice
even by the rough and ready standards of the
Mid-West.

'You got a lawyer in this town?' demanded
Brogan, when told.

'We had one once,' admitted Gordon. 'He didn't
stay too long though, said there was nothin' much
for him to do.'

'So who's gonna defend me? I got a right to a
defence lawyer.'

'Sure you have,' smiled Gordon, 'ain't nobody
sayin' as you ain't. Only thing is, there ain't no
lawyer.'

'If that's the case,' said Brogan, 'if you is gonna
have a trial you need a judge. If you ain't got no
lawyer, you ain't got no judge.'

'That's where you is wrong!' laughed Gordon. 'A
judge we have got, Judge Nathanial Gordon …'

'Gordon! Is he some relation of yours?'

'My uncle,' admitted the sheriff. 'Used to be a
Circuit Judge, but he don't do that no more, but
he's still a judge!' The sheriff laughed again.
'Don't worry yourself none about him bein' related
to me; uncle or not, he's a fair judge an' he's
promised you a fair trial before he sentences you
to hangin' – told me so himself!'

'I can well imagine just how fair it's gonna be!'
grunted Brogan. 'There don't seem a lot of point in

havin' a trial; seems I'm guilty before I start. You might just as well have a lynchin'.'

'Lynchin's against the law, even out here!' objected Gordon. 'Neither Uncle Nat nor me is gonna be party to anythin' what's against the law!' He paused and smiled slightly. 'This'll be the first hangin' we've ever had in Big Rock!' He seemed quite pleased at the prospect. 'If you look outa that window you can just see Teddy Taylor fixin' up a hangin' post ...' Brogan looked and could indeed see a wooden structure being erected. 'This time tomorrow it'll be all over an' done with. I already hear that all the folks in the territory is gonna make it some kinda public holiday.'

'I'd sure hate to disappoint 'em!' grunted Brogan. 'This Carter woman, the one I'm supposed to've raped, how is she?'

'Much the same from what I hear,' shrugged Gordon. 'I think the doc's managed to get through to her that we caught you.'

'Yeh, you caught me.' Brogan hissed, 'but you ain't caught the man what raped her!'

'So you keep on sayin'!' laughed Gordon. 'But then you would, wouldn't you, it's your neck what's gonna be stretched ain't it?' He laughed loudly and returned to his desk where he rummaged through some drawers, eventually frowning and looking hard at his prisoner. 'I've been through all my wanted posters, but I can't seem to find one on you. What you say your name was?'

'McNally, Brogan McNally – an' you is wastin' your time lookin'! I ain't wanted nowhere for nothin', never have been.'

'Find that hard to believe,' shrugged Gordon. 'I guess you've just been lucky.'

'Not lucky, just honest!' rasped Brogan. 'Send a wire through to Apache Falls, they'll tell all about how I got rid of an outlaw called Clem Cartwright an' his cronies for 'em.'

'We ain't got no telegraph!' said Gordon, at which Brogan was not surprised. 'Apache Falls? Yeh, I heard of it, ain't never been there though. So you reckon you got rid of a bunch of outlaws. Okay, maybe you did an' maybe you didn't. That'd sure account for why a saddlebum's got almost $300 on him; most normal folk can't afford to carry that kind of money. More likely you stole it, probably from Widder Carter, but we don't know that yet. What you say the name of this outlaw was?'

'Cartwright, Clem Cartwright!'

Sheriff Gordon rummaged through his posters again. 'Yeh, here he is, Clem Cartwright, $3000 dead or alive. Wanted for murder, bank robbery an' rape. You reckon he's dead?'

'No, he escaped.'

'An' I suppose you is tailin' him?'

Brogan shook his head. 'No, can't say as I was. Far as I know he headed up north-east.'

'Too bad!' smiled Gordon. 'Maybe it'd been better if he had headed this way, you could've claimed it was him.' Brogan whole-heartedly agreed with the sentiment.

'Any chance of some food?' Brogan asked as the sheriff appeared to be packing up for the night.

'Food! That'd be a waste of good cookin'!' came

the mocking reply. 'One thing's for certain, it ain't starvation you is gonna die of!' He stomped out and locked the office door and Brogan could only assume that he was to get no food.

He sat quietly for a time, pondering over his situation and weighing up the possibilities; he had been in some tight spots before, but never with the law and he had to admit that his position looked rather hopeless.

'You ain't never had need to pray before,' he said to himself, 'reckon you could start now?'

'Can't see it makin' much difference,' he replied. 'Sheriff an' judge both got their victim, that's all they is interested in.'

'Exactly! Can't hurt none to pray though, even if you ain't never believed in nothin' before. Just maybe there is somethin'.'

'An' you expect whoever, or whatever there is, to listen to you now, just 'cos we is in a tight corner? More'n like He'll just say "Tough luck, you shoulda believed before, serves you right". Kinda like a bank manager, he ain't gonna lend no money if he don't know you an' you ain't got no collateral.'

'Guess so!' he shrugged.

The hurriedly arranged court was to be held in the saloon, which gave most of the ladies an excuse to sample a few of the delights normally frowned upon and, before Judge Nathanial Gordon had taken his seat, most of the townsfolk had greatly depleted the stock in the saloon, which pleased the owner very much. When the judge did appear, he too gave the impression of having taken the opportunity to make sure that his throat was well lubricated.

'All rise!' commanded the sheriff as the judge entered the room. 'Silence in court!' He felt that he had to say that, even though there was a deathly, expectant hush in the room; he had read it somewhere.

The old judge, complete in threadbare gown, surveyed those assembled with what he fondly imagined was an official gaze – in reality more of an alcoholic haze – rapped the table with a gavel and sat down.

'Bring in the accused!' he commanded.

'He's already here!' whispered his nephew, the sheriff, pointing at Brogan.

'Hmmmph!' muttered the judge. 'Name?'

'McNally ...' replied Brogan, about to launch into his own defence.

'McNally!' interrupted the judge. 'Knew a McNally years ago; any relation, back in New York that was?'

'Not as far as I know ...'

'Don't matter none!' interrupted the judge again. 'McNally, you're charged with rapin' an' beatin' the widow Carter. How do you plead, guilty or not guilty?'

'Not guilty ...' replied Brogan, about to start again.

'Rubbish!' snapped the judge. 'Open an' shut case! From what I hear you were caught in the act ...'

'No he wasn't!' said Sheriff Gordon, a little to Brogan's surprise. 'We caught him just after, tryin' to fool us he was ...' His evidence was stopped short by a movement at the saloon doors and everyone turned to see a heavily-bandaged woman being wheeled in in an ancient bathchair, pushed by a well-dressed, middle-aged man, who turned out to be the doctor.

'She insisted on bein' here!' the doctor said, almost apologetically. 'She's much better this mornin' but I tried to talk her out of it but she wouldn't listen. She's made a remarkable recovery since I told her you'd caught him. She says she wants to see him hanged.'

'You've got that right,' said the judge. 'Bring her to the front, that is if you can bear to look at the man what so cruelly treated you, Mrs Carter!'

'I'll spit in his face!' rasped a voice from under the bandages, as she was pushed forward. The sheriff indicated Brogan, who was now standing up, and Mrs Carter looked at him for a few moments, turning her head slightly. 'Who's he?' she said, eventually.

'McNally, the man who attacked you,' said the sheriff.

'He may be called McNally,' rasped Mrs Carter, 'but he sure ain't the bastard who attacked me. I ain't never seen this feller in my life before ...' A loud buzz filled the room and everyone looked at each other, almost disappointed. 'He's about the same build, but that's all!'

'You mean this ain't the man?' asked Judge Gordon, leaning forward in disbelief. 'You've had a nasty experience, Mrs Carter, maybe your memory ain't what it was.'

'It's my face an' body that was knocked about!' rasped Mrs Carter. 'There's nothin' wrong with my memory. I ain't never set eyes on this feller before!'

'It's gotta be the shock of what he did!' protested Sheriff Gordon. 'You ain't got no need to be scared, there ain't nothin' he can do now!'

'He ain't the feller!' insisted Mrs Carter. 'Get it into your thick head, Michael Gordon, it ain't the feller!'

General pandemonium broke loose and people raced outside to tell those who could not get inside what had happened and Brogan could only smile with relief.

'Maybe there is somebody up there!' he said to himself, raising his eyes upwards and smiling. He went forward to Mrs Carter and clasped her hand. 'Ma'am,' he said, sincerely, 'I ain't never been so glad to see a woman before – you just saved my life!'

'You look an' smell like a saddlebum!' sniffed Mrs Carter. 'But I guess even saddlebums got a right to justice.'

In the meantime Judge Nat Gordon was trying his best to regain control of his courtroom, shouting 'Order! Order!' but to no avail and eventually he gave up trying and called out 'Case dismissed!' and motioned the bartender to bring him another drink, which he gulped down greedily.

'Guess we owe you an apology,' muttered Sheriff Gordon. 'Lucky for you she insisted on bein' here.'

'Maybe this'll teach you to check your facts first!' grunted Brogan. 'I reckon you picked on me just 'cos I'm a saddletramp an' a stranger.'

'Yeh!' admitted Gordon, grudgingly. 'You gotta admit, it sure was some coincidence though.'

'Always were a hothead!' scolded Mrs Carter.

'Well, I done my duty, I'm kinda tired ...' she looked up at the doc. 'Take me outa here; it ain't fittin' for a lady to be seen in a saloon. In the meantime, Michael Gordon, you'd better get out there an' find who really did it!'

'I got me an idea 'bout that,' said Brogan. 'Sheriff, you go fetch that poster of Clem Cartwright.'

'Cartwright! But you said he headed north-east!'

'An' I was headed for Salt Lake City, but I ended up here!' Brogan pointed out. 'Ain't no tellin' where a man like Cartwright's gonna end up.'

'It's a long shot,' agreed Gordon, grudgingly. 'Okay, Mrs Carter, can you hang on here while I go get it?'

'I ain't got no plans on goin' nowheres particular,' rasped Mrs Carter. 'Go get your poster, I'll wait.'

'Do you know this man?' asked the doc.

'I had some dealin's with him,' admitted Brogan. 'It's just the kinda thing he'd do. Real mean character.'

'Still, it ain't no concern of yours,' said Mrs Carter. 'I guess you can't wait to get the hell outa this place.'

'I've had better welcomes,' admitted Brogan, ruefully. 'First time I've ever been accused of anythin' like this.'

'Most drifters got somethin' they ain't proud of,' said Mrs Carter, 'but I got me this feelin' you ain't one of 'em.'

'I ain't never done no harm to nobody what don't deserve it,' Brogan grinned.

Sheriff Gordon returned with a handful of posters and handed them to Mrs Cartwright, leaving

Clem Cartwright's picture until last; she picked it out immediately.

'That's him! Good likeness too.'

Brogan sighed. 'Seems I can't get rid of him. I oughta just ride out an' leave you to it, but I feel beholden to find him.'

'Ain't no need!' huffed the sheriff, not liking the thought that someone else might succeed where he had failed.

'I know there ain't no need,' said Brogan, 'but this is now kinda personal.'

'Okay,' sighed the sheriff, 'be glad of your help, you can join the posse.'

'I don't join no posses,' smiled Brogan. 'A man like that'd hear a posse comin' a couple of miles off an' you'd never be able to find him.'

'An' you would?' sneered Gordon.

'Yeh,' said Brogan, simply but sincerely.

'I ain't tryin' to tell you your job,' said Mrs Carter, 'but I'd start at my place if I was you.'

'Just what I intended to do,' smiled Brogan.

Having been given his horse, guns and money back, Brogan followed the instructions to Mrs Carter's homestead, which lay about four miles east of the town in a wide, shallow valley. There seemed little to recommend the area to anyone, but then he had seen some homesteads in some very peculiar places.

The building itself was rather rundown, obviously it had seen better days and at first he found the task of locating signs of Cartwright very difficult, since there had obviously been a great many other horses milling about quite recently. Brogan mentally cursed what he assumed to be the posse and immediately widened his scope. After about ten minutes he discovered the tell-tale signs of a lone horse heading up into the low hills to the north of the valley. Following them proved quite easy, especially to him. Where other eyes may not have noticed the signs, with his years of experience they stood out like beacons.

Two hours later he came upon a recently used camp site and he judged that the embers of the fire were not much more than six hours old. It was apparent that Cartwright, if it was Cartwright, had spent the night there and was now set on a north-westerly course.

Sheriff Gordon had wasted no time in organizing a posse and, knowing the terrain, had decided on a course more or less due north from Big Rock. Whether or not he would be able to cut off Cartwright would be largely a matter of good fortune and Brogan was not too worried about it.

He rode for another five hours, passing through largely barren, rocky land, but he was able to follow the trail quite easily. He reasoned that the rider ahead of him would not be on the lookout for anyone following and certainly not a lone rider, so he felt it safe to proceed. The last person Cartwright would be expecting would be Brogan and even if he did see him, he probably would not be able to recognize him. He also reasoned that he would have to stop and rest his horse somewhere, so he kept a lookout for likely places.

After five hours, the terrain began to change; there was slightly more about in the way of grass and shrubs, which indicated that water was not too much of a problem and he fully expected to find the trail stopping at a water-hole. His assumption proved correct, he found signs of a very recent fire near a large pool.

A quick check told him that his quarry had left fairly recently, continuing his journey north-west, but Brogan too decided that his old horse deserved a rest and settled down by the water-hole. He was in no hurry, he would catch up with Cartwright, he was quite certain of that.

He had been there perhaps an hour, he was not too sure since he had dozed off and roundly cursed himself for doing so. His senses were screaming at him and he never disregarded his senses – his own logic and that of his horse, which often seemed to have more logic than he did, yes – but never his senses.

There was nothing to be seen, nothing to be heard, but all was not right, even his horse was uneasy. 'You heard somethin', old girl?' he whispered to her and she tossed her head in seeming affirmation. 'I ain't heard nothin', but I got this feelin' we is bein' watched.' Again, she tossed her head.

He tried not to give the impression of having been alerted, but his keen eyes scanned the surrounding rocks for the slightest sign of life, any signal, no matter how slight that would locate the watcher he knew to be there.

He saw the movement a fraction of a second before a shot echoed round the rocks and a bullet thudded into the ground close to his body. The movement had been slight, but it had meant that he had been able to move just enough to avoid the bullet. Where it thudded into the earth, his body had been lying a split second earlier.

His lightning reaction and roll to the cover of a large rock all happened in a split second and the rock saved him from another bullet. With the second shot, he was able to pinpoint exactly where his assailant was, although he had been pretty certain the first time. His problems were that now he was confined to the small hollow which contained the water-hole and he was unable to get a clear shot in return. He had taken the precaution of having his rifle with him, he almost always did under such circumstances.

'Never figured on seein' you again!' called a familiar voice. 'Glad I did though, I'm gonna kill you, you interferin' bastard!'

'An' I didn't figure on meetin' up with you again, Cartwright!' called Brogan. 'Last I heard you was headin' north-east, towards Albuquerque!'

'Changed my mind!' laughed Cartwright. 'I figured they'd know who I was up there. Glad I did too, now I got you just where I want you. You ain't got nowheres to run an' there ain't no stupid dam you can blow this time either!' Brogan was forced to agree that he was not in a very healthy position – again! 'It's just you an' me this time, bum, an' you ain't got no chance!'

'Wouldn't be too sure 'bout that!' called Brogan, more in bravado than anything else. 'There's a posse out lookin' for you.'

'Posse! Shit on the posse!' shouted Cartwright. 'Where from?'

'Place called Big Rock, just about four miles from where you raped that woman!'

'You heard 'bout that? She still alive?'

'Yeh, I heard about it,' called Brogan, 'an' she's still alive, was able to identify you from your Wanted poster.'

'Shoulda killed the cow!' laughed Cartwright. 'Damned near did I reckon.'

'Yeh, you damned near did, but she's still alive. What you wanna do somethin' stupid like that for?'

'Mighty fine woman,' called Cartwright, 'an' it's been a long time since I had me a woman!'

'Still a stupid thing to do,' sneered Brogan. 'You got enough money on you to have you a woman in any town you like. You could even have had old Maud from the stagin'-post, all part of the service.'

'I may not have had a woman in a long time, but even I'm particular!' laughed Cartwright. 'I'd say she was more your type than mine! So what you doin' out here? Heard I was around so decided to come and try to get your money back?'

'I got my money back from Apache Falls, but I could always use some more. All the men what was with you is either dead or in jail now, won't be long before you join 'em.'

'Dead or in jail?' came the mocking question.

'Don't bother me none which,' replied Brogan. 'Seems to me we got somethin' of a stalemate. I can't get you an' you'd never get close enough to get me!'

'I can wait!' sneered Cartwright. 'You is holed up where you are, me, I can be anywhere, you'll never know just where!'

'We can't stay here forever,' called Brogan. 'It's gonna be a case of who either cracks or gets fed up first!'

'Like I say, I can wait!' laughed Cartwright. With that Brogan sensed that he had changed his position and took the opportunity to hide himself a little better.

There was another shot from Cartwright, about ten minutes later, but Brogan knew that it was meant simply to tell him that he was still around although he could not see him. It was towards dusk when Brogan suddenly sat up slightly, alert to another, distant sound. In the time-honoured fashion, using a method he had learned from the Indians, he lowered his head to the ground and listened.

When he did this most people laughed at him, but it worked, at least for him, and he reckoned he could hear horses up to a mile off. Whether it was that far was questionable, but he could certainly hear them fairly close to. This time he detected the rumble of many hooves and smiled slightly, realizing that it must be the posse led by Sheriff Gordon and they seemed to be headed his way. He decided to give them something to guide them.

Raising his rifle, he fired at a rock, behind which he suspected Cartwright was hidden. The shot echoed around and Cartwright called out.

'Better luck next time, bum! Looks like it's you what's crackin' up first!' There was another shot from Cartwright which thudded close to where Brogan was, but he was in no immediate danger. However, Cartwright's shot must have had the effect of alerting the approaching riders. Brogan listened to the ground again and could hear nothing, so he had to assume that they had heard it.

'Your time is almost up!' called Brogan, sending another guiding shot aimlessly into the air.

'My time!' scorned Cartwright, from somewhere behind him. 'I'd say you got that wrong somehow.'

'We'll see!' laughed Brogan.

There was silence for about another ten minutes but suddenly Brogan was aware of movement directly in front of him, not just one but at least two, which meant that it was not Cartwright. The sense of relief was almost overwhelming, but he still made no attempt to move, just in case.

'That you, McNally?' The voice of Sheriff Gordon echoed around.

'Yeh, it's me!' called Brogan. 'that you Sheriff?'

'Yeh, heard the shootin',' came the reply. 'We was on our way back. It's okay, you can come out, we've got Cartwright.'

Brogan eased himself up, still a little wary. 'I didn't hear no shootin'!'

'Didn't need to,' laughed Gordon. 'Gave himself up as sweet as a newborn baby, especially when he saw ten guns pointed at him.'

Brogan stood up and walked out into the open just as Sheriff Gordon slithered down a slope towards him. 'I heard you comin',' said Brogan, 'that's why I gave you a couple of shots to make sure you'd heard.'

'Don't know if I believe that or not,' laughed Gordon. 'Don't matter none anyhow, we got Cartwright, that's all that matters.'

'He's admitted he raped Mrs Carter,' said Brogan.

'Yeh, admitted it to us too. You comin' back to town?'

'Thanks, no,' laughed Brogan. 'I just about had me enough of your hospitality for the moment. He should have a load of money on him; by rights it belongs to the folk of Apache Falls.'

'An' there's a reward of three thousand,' reminded the sheriff.

'Give my share to Mrs Carter,' said Brogan.

'Didn't say you was gettin' a share!' grinned Gordon. 'But I'll make sure she gets some of it.'

Brogan went to where they were holding Clem Cartwright and smiled sardonically. 'I guess it was you what cracked first.'

'The devil himself must be lookin' after you!' snarled Cartwright.

'Yeh, maybe he is!' laughed Brogan. 'Maybe he is!'